DEATH OF A LITURGIST

DEATH OF A LITURGIST

LORRAINE V. MURRAY

Saint Benedict Press
Charlotte, North Carolina

ISBN: 978-1-935302-46-9

Cover art and design by Tony Pro.

Printed and Bound in the United States of America

SAINT BENEDICT PRESS

Saint Benedict Press
Charlotte, North Carolina
2010

For Julie and Charles Anderson

Acknowledgments

One of an author's greatest blessings is a wise editor, so my deepest thanks go to Todd Aglialoro at Saint Benedict Press for his many ingenious improvements on the manuscript. I am also grateful to Chris Harvey, my friend in law enforcement, who answered my questions about police work. And I can never sufficiently thank my dear husband, Jeffrey Murray, for encouraging me and providing me with homemade wine and chocolates as needed.

Chapter 1

"Good morning! Have you been saved?"

Francesca Bibbo peered through her screen door, wishing she had ignored the bell. There on her front porch stood three heavyset women, perspiring heavily and fanning themselves. All had chocolate-colored skin, blue-black hair twisted into determined braids, and smiles that revealed dazzling, perfectly aligned teeth. Despite the thick heat of the Georgia summer, they were decked out in dresses, high heels, and large hats from which sprang gardens of jaunty silk flowers.

"Uh, yes, that is, I think . . . ," Francesca began, and then immediately regretted the note of hesitation in her voice.

She was a Roman Catholic who faithfully attended Mass, received the Sacraments, and tried to love her fellow man—even the ones who rang her doorbell at nine on a Friday morning.

Does that count as saved?

"I'm Mother Rosetta, and these are my girls, Earnestine and Wanda." The oldest of the three women, who had to weigh well over 200 pounds, fanned herself even more vigorously. Little streams of sweat trickled down her plump cheeks, and a yellow rose on her hat trembled. She moved her face so close that Francesca could see the constellation of freckles that peppered the bridge of her nose.

"Honey, do you know Jesus Christ?"

Francesca wished she weren't wearing a bathrobe and pink pig slippers complete with a curly tail. *They're not going to take me very seriously.*

"Yes, of course, you see, I'm a Catholic and I . . ."

Now the smiles on the three women's faces collapsed. They looked at each other nervously, as if Francesca had just announced she was an axe murderer. Mother Rosetta reached into a large handbag and extracted a small copy of the New Testament.

"This is the word of God, sugar." She spoke slowly, as if addressing someone who didn't understand English.

"This will teach you about Jesus Christ and how He died on the Cross for you."

Francesca felt a mosquito sinking its proboscis into her right ankle. She knew she had a choice—engage the three women in a theological debate or make a quick getaway and hunt down the mosquito.

"Thanks so much. I'll be sure to read it." Francesca quickly opened the door, accepted the little book with a smile, and then took a swipe at her ankle. But she could tell by the expression on Mother Rosetta's face that there was more to come.

"Our church is just four miles from here, honey, and me and my girls invite you to join us any Sunday at 11. That's when we gather to worship and praise the Lord."

The mosquito was feasting on Francesca's other ankle. She began hopping up and down as she tried to swat it while also trying to look interested in the invitation.

"Uh, thanks so much. I already go to a church in Decatur, Saint Rita's, but if I get a chance, I will come by."

"You be sure to do that, honey," Mother Rosetta said. "You come on over to God's Truth Tabernacle and worship with us. The spirit really gets moving there, doesn't it, girls?"

Earnestine and Wanda nodded their heads vigorously, and the flowers on their hats danced. And then their mother added the punch line: "We'll be back to see you, sugar, real soon!"

Francesca closed the door gratefully and rubbed her ankles. *If anyone doubts this is a fallen world, just come down to Georgia where we have mosquitoes year-round.* Then she stooped down to pet Tubs, her old arthritic white cat that sported a black patch on his back shaped like Africa. His favorite pastime was looking out the window and making threatening noises at birds. The few times she had allowed him access to the yard, however, he had returned quickly to the front porch, where he had sat meowing nervously until she let him back in.

After the missionaries were gone, Francesca basked for a few moments in the thick silence—until a huge concrete mixer truck began grinding out an ear-splitting din at the neighbors' house across the way. The new neighbors had already repaved the driveway twice in one year. They evidently had some platonic ideal of what cement should look like and would continue striving toward their dream until they achieved it.

The phone rang. "I have a tidbit of rather shocking information for you." Rebecca Goodman's voice shot across the line eagerly without even an opening greeting.

Rebecca was a friend from the choir at Saint Rita's Church near the town square in Decatur and a member of the Choir Chicks, a group Francesca had founded. She was five foot three, about the same height as Francesca, but much heavier. With her fine, smooth skin and thick, honey-blonde hair, Rebecca was one of those overweight women condemned to be told by well-meaning relatives that she had "such a pretty face." She taught fifth grade at Saint Rita's school and desperately wanted to get married. In fact, she had told her friends that her biological clock wasn't just ticking but had gone into full alarm mode when she had recently turned 40.

Before Francesca could comment, Rebecca delivered the big news: "We're getting a new pastor."

There was a pause, and then the real zinger: "And there's talk that the music at Saint Rita's—and lots else—is going to change drastically."

"But what will happen to Father John?"

"He's going to a small parish in Rome—and I'm talking Georgia, not Italy."

Francesca's spirits sank. Saint Rita's choir prided itself on producing dignified, traditional music at Sunday Mass. There was a Gregorian chant group that sang after Holy Communion, and there was a lovely, mystical use of many of the sung Mass responses in Latin. The idea of that changing struck a dark chord in her soul.

The music had been overseen by a choir director who was kept under the thumb of the pastor, Father John Riley, a man devoted to reverent liturgy. The director, however, had met an untimely death shortly before last Christmas. Since then, a temporary director had continued the tradition. Gregorian chants, organ music, and selections from the likes of Bach, Palestrina, Mozart, and Fauré were standard Sunday fare.

"Francesca, are you still there?"

"Sorry, I was daydreaming. I guess we should wait and see if the rumors are true. I mean, isn't it possible the new pastor might decide to keep the music at Saint Rita's the way it is? You know the saying: if it ain't broke, don't fix it."

Rebecca laughed. "Oh, sweetie, you're such an optimist. Well, maybe you're right, but the rumors right now are as thick as gnats at a South Georgia picnic."

There was a crash on the other end of the line and the sound of a child screaming. Francesca envisioned chaos breaking out among the children in Rebecca's pottery class, which she taught every summer at the YWCA.

"I have to go. The kids are throwing clay at each other," Rebecca said.

After the call, Francesca poured a cup of coffee and mused. The choir was on break for the summer, so if a new director did come on board, it would not be until the fall. But she wondered what other kinds of changes would be in store for the congregation. She would certainly miss Father John Riley, but despite Rebecca's misgivings, she decided to trust the judgment of the new pastor. She had to believe he wouldn't do anything that was tacky or irreverent. At this, Tubs let out a big meow, which she realized was not a comment but a reminder that she had forgotten to refill his bowl.

Once she had fed him, she intended to drive over to the rectory to answer phones, which was one of her volunteer projects for the church. She didn't want to leave the pastor in the lurch, even though on a hot day like this the neighborhood pool was beckoning, but thinking about Venetian Pools reminded her of her late husband, Dean. He had not been that keen on lap swimming but had enjoyed accompanying her to the pool. He liked to sink to the bottom and stay there so long that she would finally nudge him with her toes to be sure he was alive.

But her beloved had died in a car accident two years before, and her life had changed drastically since then. The only bright spot in an otherwise black sky was that he had invested wisely, and Francesca no longer had to work to make ends meet. She was only 38 but already considered herself "retired."

She hurried into the bedroom and began dressing, stopping to glance fondly at the cluster of framed photos on her dresser that showed Dean at his desk, Dean in the garden, Dean sitting with her on the front-porch swing. She picked one up, kissed the image of his face, and held the photo against her for a second. *Rest in peace, my love.*

As she brushed her hair, she gazed into the mirror with her usual critical eye. Since childhood, she had weighed a few more pounds than what the charts said was ideal for her height. She had been on numerous diets since her days as a chubby child in grade school, all to no avail, and she sometimes joked that the best solution to her weight problem would be to grow two inches. The daughter of Italian American parents, Francesca had long fretted about her nose, with its decidedly Roman shape, but once Dean had declared it cute, she had stopped wishing for a perkier model. Now she twisted her long, molasses-brown hair into a ponytail and looked carefully at her reflection. *OK, not perfect, but once I start that new exercise program, I know I'll slim down.*

* * * *

Father John Riley looked over his nearly empty room with a mixture of dismay and elation. He had all his books packed and ready to go, plus the few items he had brought with him when he had arrived at Saint Rita's seven years ago: the treasured black-and-white photo of his parents on their wedding day, the faded Polaroid of his three sisters and four brothers under a crooked Christmas tree, and the odd collection of knickknacks that he kept promising to throw away but simply couldn't.

There was the rock painted to look like a sleeping cat, which had been a gift from his eldest sister, the shell of a horseshoe crab he had found while vacationing in Cedar Key, Florida, and the herd of stuffed animals that the children at Saint Rita's had given him: scruffy mice, a large jovial chicken, a moose, and a pack of black dogs.

Oh my gosh, I almost forgot. I have to pack Spot's water dish and food. I sure hope I'm doing the right thing, taking the old mutt along with me to the new rectory. He's done plenty of damage here.

The dog, seemingly a mixture of a dozen or so breeds, had appeared at Saint Rita's rectory one day out of nowhere, and Father John had taken him in. Even though the mutt was completely black, his name tag read "Spot," and it was the only name he would answer to, so it stuck. As if on cue, the dog now roused himself from the corner, where he slept on a raggedy, odoriferous blanket, and ambled over to poke his icy nose against Father's thin sock.

"Rise and shine, Spot! Do you realize you've been sleeping for over 12 hours?" Father John joked. The dog yawned, stretched, and let out a groaning sound.

Father John was really going to miss Saint Rita's, having grown attached to the parishioners, especially the children at the accompanying school. Since he would never have children of his own, he dearly loved hearing the little ones call him "Father."

It was hard being transferred, but it was all part of a priest's job. Transfers were constant reminders that a priest's main attachment was to God, not human beings. On the other hand, as painful as it would be to leave his little flock in Decatur, he was looking forward to the parish in Rome. *It should be a slower pace*, he thought. *Fewer parishioners—and maybe fewer demands from blasted development committees.*

Now he absently handed the dog a biscuit while he began morning prayers. "Lord, open my lips, and my mouth will proclaim your praise." He said the words aloud, but his mind kept straying as he stared through the open window at a cluster of clouds sailing along in the ocean-blue sky, while in a nearby oak tree a squirrel sat with its front paws clasped as if joining him in prayer.

Father John suspected some parishioners at Saint Rita's would be eager to welcome a new pastor because they very much wanted a larger, more elaborate sanctuary, plus many other rather costly additions and improvements. Father John had resisted their demands; he just couldn't see going into debt to fine-tune a perfectly decent structure when there were so many Christians all over the world worshipping the Lord in ramshackle huts. There was an old saying: "To a man with a hammer, all the world is a nail." It seemed that any parish with a group called "development" would not be content with the status quo for long.

"Come, let us sing to the Lord and shout with joy to the Rock who saves us." Father John was beginning to wonder if

Spot knew morning prayers because at this moment each day the dog would nudge him again, and he would automatically dole out another biscuit, which the mutt devoured in seconds.

I hope the new guy won't make too many changes. All I know about him is he's supposed to be good with balancing budgets. And, thank God, he's also known to be serious about visiting the shut-ins and the dying.

Saint Rita's was located in a part of Decatur that was heavily populated with nursing homes, many sporting winsome names like "Merry Manor" and "Eternal Sunrise." A pastor had to have the energy to make daily visits to the elderly shut-ins or he wouldn't last long. Father John sighed. He knew many of the parishioners were nervous about a change in personnel. They feared that some of their traditions might be shaken up. *But this isn't my concern anymore. The situation now is right where it always has been—in the hands of God.*

Father John's ears detected the strains of a Gregorian chant recording wafting from the assistant pastor's room down the hall. The recently ordained Father William Snortland was only 30, and Father John had quickly grown fond of the pudgy, balding fellow who had truly childlike faith. Unfortunately, though, the man had a tendency to deliver provocative sermons, which often caused complaints to land on the pastor's desk.

Father John shook his head sadly as he recalled the previous Sunday, when the young priest had told the congregation that the money they spent on gourmet food for their pets should go to the poor. He absently handed Spot another biscuit. *Of course, what William said was true, but it wasn't a message animal lovers wanted to hear. And I've been dealing with the fallout.* Still, the young man was a compassionate soul who often visited the residents of four nursing homes and patients at two nearby hospitals all in one day.

* * * *

As she drove over to Saint Rita's, Francesca felt a twinge of guilt. The church was about two miles from her house, and she knew she should be walking for the exercise. But as she glanced outside at the big, egg-yolk-yellow sun that seemed intent on burning a hole in the thin blue sky, she felt trickles of sweat forming on her brow even with the air-conditioner running full blast.

Driving just makes more sense on a day like this, she assured herself. She tried to ignore the other voice that chimed in: *Yes, but you also drive even when the weather is perfect.*

Shut up and leave me alone, she countered. That ended the argument. She parked quickly and then settled in at her desk in the downstairs foyer of the rectory near the kitchen. Then she rummaged in the drawer for her lapel pin, which proclaimed, "Don't yell at me—I'm just a volunteer." Attaching it to her blouse, she felt the mild rumbling sensation that signaled that a subway train had just zoomed underneath. The church had been built in a fairly peaceful section of downtown Decatur, but when the city decided to add the subway line, some planner had decided that the route should go right under the church. Although most longtime parishioners had eventually grown accustomed to the rumblings, she still found the situation unnerving. She was also well aware of complaints from the housekeeper who had to go around righting crooked pictures on the wall after they had been slowly bumped off-kilter by the tremors.

Francesca liked volunteering at the church, but today she was melancholy. Memories of her late husband filled her head. She had refused to take her friends' advice to sell their house in Chelsea Heights, where they had lived so happily during the 15 years of their marriage. She just couldn't see leaving behind all the reminders of her sweetheart. Dean had planted muscadine vines and fig trees in the yard. He'd also fashioned a wooden screen door that featured a large oak tree with a squirrel perched on a branch.

It had been difficult to start dating again after his death. At first she had felt like she was cheating on him. But recently she had met a good-looking, never-married homicide detective named Tony Viscardi. They were dating steadily, but she was not eager to jump into marriage without being completely sure he was "the one." So far, just having a man to talk with was enough.

She straightened out the desk and began inserting announcement sheets into the Sunday bulletins. As she did, the phone lines began flashing. *Like lightning bugs in the Okefenokee Swamp.* Three weeks had passed since news of Father John's leaving had been announced to the congregation. Some parishioners had been out of town for his farewell luncheon, and they were eager to say their good-byes. She put through as many calls as possible but had to take messages from some.

The kitchen door swung open and in walked the housekeeper and cook, Maria Grabowski. "It must be 100 degrees out there," she announced, pulling out a large flowery handkerchief and mopping her moist brow.

Still on the phone, Francesca just nodded, while Maria rummaged around in a purse so big it could easily have concealed a pot roast, finally extracting a lipstick and a small mirror. Seemingly oblivious to the fact that Francesca was on the phone, Maria continued, "They had these lipsticks on sale over at Walgreens, so I bought three." She giggled. "They're called 'Perfect Passion,' whatever that is."

Francesca watched as Maria painted her plump lips a deep vermillion. Then she rooted around in her purse a bit more and produced a cluster of index cards with recipes written on them.

The phones finally went silent. "You look a little down this morning, honey. Anything wrong?" Maria asked.

Maria was a thin, tanned, slightly muscular woman in her midthirties who wore her blonde hair in little spikes poking up at odd angles from her head. At times, her exuberant mannerisms and unedited comments had proven a bit much for some of the previous pastors, but Francesca figured no one dared fire her. After all, Maria's recipes, especially for pot roast, mashed potatoes, and blueberry pie, were said to be divinely inspired.

"Just a touch of the blues—nothing serious." Francesca fiddled with a pencil. She was afraid she might burst into tears if Maria probed more deeply into her emotional state.

But she needn't have worried. "Honey, the best thing for that is hot biscuits and coffee—and I'm fixin' to make a batch of biscuits right now."

Fanning herself with the cards as she spoke, Maria went on: "Father John asked me to get here early today because he wants a special welcome lunch for the new pastor. That meant I had to give my kids cereal for breakfast when I usually do waffles for them. But I'd do anything for that man. Even if he sometimes forgets to say thank you, I know he means well, bless his heart."

Maria had immigrated to the United States from Poland with her parents when she was ten, and they had settled in Macon, Georgia. She still retained heavy traces of her native tongue, and Francesca was always a bit startled to hear her using expressions like "y'all." But Maria was that rarest of beings—a Polish Southern belle.

Francesca had lived in the South all her life but had never quite achieved the status of "belle." Her parents had grown up in New York City, and she had inherited their northern accent. Still, she delighted in Maria's Southern belle-isms, especially her habits of calling nearly everyone "sugar" or "honey" and saying "bless his heart" after criticizing anyone.

Maria scurried into the kitchen, and soon Francesca could hear pots clanging and dishes rattling, accompanied by low murmuring sounds, which she knew were Maria saying the Rosary aloud. It was rumored that the splendid dishes Maria turned out were only partly due to the cache of secret recipes stored in her voluminous handbag: some said it was the constant stream of prayers that created pie crust so tender it brought tears to the eyes and fried chicken so crisp that a spout of delicate steam rose from the sweet flesh when you took the first bite.

* * * *

Upstairs, Father William was wrapping a small good-bye gift for the pastor. My *first boss*, he thought sadly. *I wonder what the new one will be like. I hope he'll be as conservative in running the parish as Father John was, but you never know.*

Father William and Father John favored a reverent approach to Mass and a firm line when it came to doctrine. Both were opposed to the trend of segregating parishioners based on age, and so they had resisted launching teen Masses. Father William smiled as he recalled Father John's explanation to a parishioner: "We wouldn't want to have Masses that only served the elderly, would we? Or Masses for people in their forties?"

I don't know much about the new pastor, but I sure hope he follows in Father John's footsteps.

As he put the final touches on the package, which contained a leather edition of one of the pastor's favorite books, *The Imitation of Christ*, he heard a chirping sound from across the room. He went over to the large aquarium that sat near the window and looked inside. His hamster, Ignatius, was evidently talking in his sleep. *I wonder what hamsters dream about.*

Chapter 2

As Father Brent Bunt pulled into the driveway of Saint Rita's rectory, he noticed that the cement was darkly stained. The front door of the rectory had deep grooves along the bottom as if some animal had been clawing to get in. The rectory itself needed a coat of paint, and the lawn was shaggy. Climbing out of the car, he nearly stepped into a pile of dog droppings. *My work is cut out for me here, obviously.*

He rang the front doorbell and heard from within heavy sounds of scampering and something scratching on the inside of the door. An attractive woman with dark hair opened the door for him, while simultaneously bending down to grab the collar of the eager black dog that seemed intent on knocking him over.

"Don't worry, Father, he doesn't bite," the woman said.

Father Bunt cringed. He had heard this before from numerous dog owners who didn't seem to realize that in the world of canines there is always a first time. He was not a big fan of dogs or cats—or any indoor animals, for that matter—because he hated brushing off fur from his black garments. Whenever he had visited parishioners in his last parish, he had always dreaded sitting on couches that had recently been vacated by drooling, shedding pets. Invariably, he had to send his clothes to the dry cleaner's the next day.

"Spot, sit!" But the dog evidently didn't understand the woman's simple command, for he continued trying to lunge at Father Bunt's legs.

Then the woman introduced herself, and Father Bunt thought she said her name was Francesca Ditto. At that moment, he saw Father John Riley hurry into the vestibule. He didn't know the man well, but they had attended a few archdiocesan functions together. With a firm gesture, Father John derailed the dog's attempts to greet Father Bunt and clipped a leash on its collar.

"Very sorry about that," Father John said. "We're still trying to train the old boy. This is Francesca Bibbo, one of our volunteers."

"Pleased to meet you." Father Bunt extended his hand.

Just then he spied a blonde woman with wild-looking hair bustling out of the kitchen, her face and apron lightly dusted with traces of flour. Before he knew what had happened, the woman launched herself toward him and wrapped her arms firmly around his shoulders.

"Welcome to Saint Rita's," she boomed as she planted a garlic-scented kiss on his cheek.

Feeling blood rushing into his face, Father Bunt extricated himself from the woman's embrace with as much grace as possible.

"And you are?"

"Maria Grabowski, the cook and housekeeper. Please call me Maria, Father."

She stood there beaming at him as if he were her firstborn son returning from a war. Father Bunt smiled uncomfortably and tried to be as discreet as possible as he brushed off the traces of flour she had left on his clothing. He also could feel a sticky smudge of lipstick on his cheek, and he was just about to reach for a handkerchief when the cook beat him to it. She pulled a big flowery handkerchief from her apron pocket and began vigorously scrubbing at his cheek as he stood paralyzed with embarrassment.

"Bless your heart! We don't want you to get a reputation for chasing after the ladies!"

"I, er, uh . . ." He couldn't imagine how he would complete the sentence.

Father Bunt was relieved at that moment to spot a young, stocky priest hurrying down the stairs, carrying what appeared to be an aquarium. Evidently noticing the gathering by the front door, the young priest immediately put down the aquarium and introduced himself as Father William. After shaking hands, Father William excused himself and promised he would be right back.

"I'm just heading outside to clean out the hamster's habitat."

Hamsters, dogs, Father Bunt thought. *Is this a rectory or a zoo?*

* * * *

After meeting Father Bunt, Francesca returned to her desk, where the first call that came in was from Rebecca.

"Did you meet him yet?" Rebecca's voice was dripping with curiosity.

Francesca whispered into the phone, "Yes, just now. He seems very nice."

"Is he an old guy or what?"

Francesca looked around nervously to make sure Father Bunt was out of earshot. She could hear him in the kitchen, where Maria was evidently interrogating him on his favorite meals.

"Really, I'm good with whatever you cook," Francesca heard him say, and then she heard Maria: "Well, that's what Father John said, bless his heart, but the first time I cooked up a batch of country-style fried chicken livers, he looked at them like I was serving possum or something."

"I would say he's in his midforties." Francesca cupped her hand around the phone. "He's about medium height and has dark brown hair . . . some patches of gray . . ."

"Does he have a comb-over?" Rebecca interjected.

"A what?"

"You know, a few strands of hair artfully placed over a bald spot."

Francesca had to laugh. "No, nothing like that. He's rather attractive, if you want to know."

"What? I can't hear you."

Francesca raised her voice. "He's rather ATTRACTIVE."

Then she looked up and saw Father Bunt standing inches from her desk.

"Uh, thanks for calling—I have to go now," she announced gaily and hung up the phone. "Father, do you need anything?"

"Yes, do you have a copy of the bulletin for next Sunday?"

She handed him one and hoped her face wasn't flaming with embarrassment.

* * * *

Father Bunt had barely been at his new job for two days before every parishioner with a complaint or suggestion came forth to grab the ear of the flock's new shepherd. He had never served at a parish as large as Saint Rita's, and his stomach lurched each time the phone rang.

"Hello, Father, welcome to Saint Rita's! I'm Jack Davis, chair of the development committee. We sure would like to get together with you to talk about doing some work on the sanctuary and the rectory."

"Work?" he echoed with trepidation. Work usually meant major construction, and that meant fund-raising.

"Yes, you've probably noticed that the sanctuary is rather crowded. We'd like to tear down the back wall and get more room for pews. And the rectory . . . well, I'm sure you'll agree it needs plenty of renovations."

Father Bunt rubbed his forehead. *He should have seen the last rectory I lived in. Makes this one look like a palace.*

"Well, what are your estimates for these projects?" Father Bunt asked.

"Uh, why don't we get together and go over the figures in person?"

I thought so. It must run into the millions, and he doesn't want to drop the bomb over the phone.

"Yes, of course, let me check my calendar and call you back." But Father Bunt had no sooner put down the phone than Francesca put through another call.

"Father, welcome to our parish. I'm Myra Small, and I've been a parishioner here for 30 years."

Before he could say a word, she launched right in. "I know you're busy, so I'll come right to the point. Father, we need more parking. Just the other day, I had to circle the building for ten minutes looking for a space."

"Yes, well, I certainly will . . . ," he began, but she cut him off.

"And in the summer, the air conditioning just doesn't get the church cool enough. In the winter, we freeze to death."

"Ah, yes, the heating and air conditioning system." He picked up a pencil and added them to his list, while absently doodling a few big dollar signs. "I will certainly look into these concerns."

When he had a break, he logged into the parish's bank account to check on the special building fund. There was a little over $200,000 in there, meant for a new roof, carpeting, and various minor improvements. It was a hefty sum, but if the people started clamoring for more changes, it wouldn't go very far. He remembered there was a parish council report on the matter that he was supposed to read.

Just as he was jotting down some figures, the calls started up again. There were people who wanted changes in the liturgy, and others who insisted that it stay the same.

"Why can't we have special teen Masses?" one caller wanted to know.

"Well, it's possible, of course, if enough people want them."

"Father John just didn't want to go there," the caller said.

"Don't give in to those people who want teen Masses," said another. "Saint Rita's is known for traditional liturgy. We don't want electric guitars and all that."

After assuring his parishioners that he would give thoughtful reflection to their concerns, Father Bunt felt a headache developing. Just then, Margaret Hennessy, the director of religious education, stopped in. She was a tall woman in her sixties with a cheery smile and friendly brown eyes that reminded him of his childhood beagle.

"Having a hard day?" Little crinkly lines formed around her eyes.

"It's just a steady stream of parishioners. Some are desperate to get something changed—and others want things to stay the same. I guess I should have seen it coming."

She stood there with an expectant look on her face.

"Uh, Mrs. Hennessy, is there something you need?"

"Oh, please call me Margaret. I just wondered if you wanted to see the list of speakers for our next RCIA program."

"Is that something you usually handle?"

"Yes, but sometimes Father John liked to see who the speakers were."

"OK, then, if you put the list on my desk, I'll take a look."

Margaret smiled and laid a piece of paper atop his overflowing in-box.

"Don't forget to stop downstairs for coffee and some biscuits, Father, when you get a chance."

"Well, thank you. Uh, Mrs. . . . Margaret, I have a note here indicating that you plan to retire in about two weeks. Is that right?"

"Yes, Father, I guess it's time. I've been here 25 years. Of course, I love my job, but I have four grandchildren now, and I can't wait to spend more time with them."

He smiled. "Well, would you do me a favor, then? Would you write me a description of your duties and we'll run an ad in the *Georgia Bulletin*?"

She rummaged around in the pile of papers she was carrying. "I've already done it. I figured you'd need it."

* * * *

The voice on the other end was a very energetic baritone.

"Father Bunt, my name is Chip Cambio. I just read your ad in the *Georgia Bulletin*, and I believe I can help you out with some responsibilities at your parish."

It had been two weeks since he'd placed the ad, and the pile of résumés was growing taller each day, but Father Bunt just hadn't found time to go through them.

"Well, Mr. Cambio, have you mailed in your résumé?"

"No, Father, I felt I should talk with you first. You see, I know you advertised for a director of religious education, but I can do a lot more than a DRE. Besides religious education, I can handle the music, oversee Christmas and Easter programs, and generally relieve some of the pressure on the pastor. For example, I help with planning marriages, getting Baptisms in order . . . that kind of thing."

A liturgist. Father Bunt swallowed hard. He had heard good and bad about them over the years but had never used one before. *But I've also never been in charge of such a big parish. This could be a godsend.*

"Why don't you fax me your résumé, Mr. Cambio, and then I'll take a look and we can get together and talk?"

When he read the résumé later that day, he was impressed. The man definitely had experience, working as a liturgist in several churches in north Florida, and a solid background in theology—including a year in the seminary. He had provided a list of references from prior parishes. Everything looked in order.

Father Bunt knew that hiring a liturgist could prove controversial. But he could already see that his time at Saint Rita's would be filled to the brim with the day-to-day tasks of running the parish: overseeing the budget, visiting the sick and dying, celebrating Mass, writing sermons, attending meetings, and administering Sacraments. With a congregation this large, he would be kept extremely busy with weddings, funerals, Baptisms, confessions, and school functions.

There was a secretary who helped run the church office, plus a housekeeper and a custodian. But it was clear what the parish was lacking. Father Bunt picked up the phone and made an appointment to interview Chip Cambio the following day.

* * * *

Father Bunt was in his office the next day by 8 a.m. sharp. He had skipped breakfast so he could interview Cambio before his next meeting at nine. Now the heady scent of fresh biscuits and sausage patties emanated from the downstairs kitchen, causing his mouth to water. His stomach was rumbling by the time he heard the firm knock on his door. *I should get this over with quickly so I can grab a bite before the meeting.*

The man who walked into the office made a confident, professional appearance. Chip Cambio had an athletic build and an even tan. He was taller than Father Bunt, maybe six feet, with a full head of close-cropped, wiry brown hair and a well-trimmed beard. His suit and tie looked expensive, and his black shoes were polished to a mirror gloss.

"It's a pleasure to meet you, Father Brent." Chip extended his hand. There was a whiff of spicy aftershave. The handshake was solid and vigorous. *Another good sign.*

Father Bunt pointed to the chair in front of his desk, and Chip sat down, carefully hiking his trouser legs above his shoes. Father cleared his throat loudly to cover up the rumbling sounds of his stomach. He picked up Chip's résumé and also glanced at the big clock on the wall.

"Well, Chip, your résumé is very impressive. I also see you were in the seminary for a while. What happened to make your plans change?"

The man adjusted what looked like an expensive watch on his left wrist. "The short answer, Father, is that I got to a point where I realized that as much as I wanted to be a priest—in terms of the Mass and the Sacraments, you know—I felt that someday I would like to get married and have a family."

Father Bunt glanced at the man's left hand, where there was no wedding ring. The man must have noticed this because he added, "I'm still looking for the right woman."

"Of course, I understand." Father studied the résumé while his stomach rumbled in protest.

"Well, Chip, you seem to have plenty of experience, so I don't think we have to drag this interview out. Why don't you tell me what you like best about your work as a liturgist?" *And make it snappy. I'm starving.*

"Father, that's a great question." Chip's voice had a pleasing ring of confidence and sincerity to it. He leaned forward and smiled, showing snowy white teeth with slightly elongated incisors.

"To be completely truthful, it's all about serving the Lord."

Father Bunt liked this direct, upbeat response. *We're going to work well together*. He licked his lips as the blissfully pungent aroma of freshly brewed coffee pervaded the room.

"When can you start?"

Chapter 3

Francesca was getting dressed for Mass while Tubs sat on an overstuffed chair in her study, watching her as she tried on outfits and then threw the discards on a nearby rocker. She could hear a Carolina wren belting out its morning song and the distinctive twitter of a hummingbird as it approached her window feeder. A few crickets chirped listlessly in the still heat of the morning.

Rummaging through her closet, she wondered what would happen to Saint Rita's choir. The temporary director had found a job elsewhere, so there would be no musical accompaniment at Mass until a new choir director was hired. When choir was in session, she sat with the altos in the choir section at the back of the church, but today she was looking forward to sitting in the pews, especially because Tony would be accompanying her to church.

She had met him while he was investigating a crime at Saint Rita's, and she had quickly felt an attraction for him. They shared an Italian ancestry, and he had certain old-fashioned qualities that appealed to her. He was the kind of man who noticed things she tended to miss—like a tire on her car that needed air or gutters on the roof crammed with leaves. He seemed to enjoy taking care of these practical matters, and that reminded her of Dean.

Tony had been raised Catholic, as she had, but, like her, had left the Church for a long time. She had come back during her marriage to Dean, but Tony's journey was still ongoing. He had begun attending Mass again only after meeting her. One evening he had told her that he was drawn to the dignity of the liturgy, especially the touches that he remembered from childhood. She recalled him listing them with a smile: Gregorian chants, the reverent hymns, the organ music, and the delicious stretch of silence that followed Holy Communion.

The doorbell rang, and she hurried to answer it. Tony came in carrying a bouquet of peach-colored roses. Even though they had been dating for a while, she was always startled by his good looks: the big espresso-colored eyes with strong brows, the olive complexion, and the dark brown hair. He was medium height like most of the men in her family, which suited her fine because she'd always felt awkward dating tall men. She found it endearing that his (definitely Italian) nose was just a bit crooked, the result of a diving accident in childhood. He had to be strong for his job with the police department, so he worked out regularly and had an appealingly muscular physique.

"When I saw these, I knew they were just right for you!" He handed her the roses and gave her a quick kiss on the cheek.

"Oh, Tony, they're . . . uh . . . they're really gorgeous."

He looked at her closely. "You don't seem very happy. You haven't developed an allergy to roses, have you?"

She laughed. "Of course not. I love them. Let me just get a vase."

As she went into the kitchen, she could hear him greeting Tubs. The old cat had taken a liking to Tony ever since the day he had brought over a cloth mouse stuffed with fresh catnip. Francesca trimmed the stems, located a vase, and filled it with water. She was delighted by the flowers but strangely saddened as well. This happened to be the exact shade of peach Dean had always chosen for her. She knew she hadn't told Tony about this, and she wondered if this coincidence held any significance.

"Penny for your thoughts." Tony took the vase from her and carried it into the living room, where he placed it next to a large framed photo of Dean.

"You look very reflective this morning," he added.

"Oh, it's nothing," she lied. "I was just thinking about how beautiful the roses are. You're so thoughtful!"

All seemed well as they entered the narthex of Saint Rita's church. There was a small crowd gathered at the back door, and she heard Father Bunt introducing a man to some of the parishioners. She heard the name "Chip Cambio" and also caught the word "liturgist." She had heard rumors that the man had been hired about a month before.

She and Tony chose the fourth pew on the right side of the church, known as Saint Joseph's side because of the big statue of the Saint that held court there. They both knelt down and crossed themselves. *Dear Lord, please take care of Dean. Please accept my Holy Communion today for the repose of his soul.* As she gazed at the statue of her favorite Saint, she found her mind straying to memories of her parents, dead for so many years.

Closing her eyes, she could see her father on the patio of their Miami home smoking one of his favorite Cuban cigars. Her mother would be in the kitchen rolling out the dough for Italian cheese pies or making *zeppole*. Wondering what Tony was praying for, Francesca glanced over at him, but his head was bowed and his eyes shut. *Please, Lord, keep Tony safe.*

Then, just as she sat back in the pew, things started going awry. A young man, his head completely shaven, walked up to the altar. His crisp shirt strained against a generous stomach as he positioned himself in front of something Francesca hadn't spotted before—a freestanding microphone.

He beamed a huge toothy smile at the congregation and tugged lightly at the knot on his tie. "Welcome to Saint Rita's! We are overjoyed that you are here to join us for our Eucharistic celebration." He paused and said something she had never heard at Saint Rita's before: "Please stand and greet the people around you."

The people near her looked surprised, but they obediently stood up and began shaking hands with each other. Francesca and Tony reluctantly followed suit, although she could see a glimmer of doubt in his eyes.

"What's going on?" he whispered, but she could only shrug.

"My name is Dwight Brown, and I will be your cantor this morning," the man announced.

It was time for the opening hymn, and she looked around for the standard hymnal, one of the sturdy *Worship II*s, the hardbound red books that housed treasured hymns from the past. But they seemed to have vanished from the pews. She could only find a paperback hymnal bound in a blue plastic folder, titled *Breaking Bread*. It had a garish abstract illustration on the cover, depicting a cross imbedded in a table with disembodied hands reaching out. She thumbed through the book quickly, noticing a few of the old favorites inside, but the majority of the songs had been written in the 1970s and 1980s.

The opening hymn was one they'd never sung before at Saint Rita's: "We Are Many Parts." Tony nudged her slightly. "Where the heck did this come from?"

"I wish I knew," she whispered back.

When it was time for the psalm, the cantor raised his arms dramatically to indicate the congregational response. Francesca tried to keep her thoughts from being uncharitable, but she automatically heard a voice in her mind chime in: *Does he think we're too dumb to know when it's our turn to sing?* She immediately uttered a silent prayer: *Please, Lord, keep me from being so judgmental.* But it was impossible to stop her critical train of thought. Someone at the back of the church was playing the piano, and the tinkling sounds reminded her of lounge music. *I didn't even know we had a piano.*

The congregation was accustomed to a long stretch of quiet after Communion, but today Dwight filled the silence with his solo rendition of "Rain Down." The man sang with great enthusiasm, "We who revere and find hope in our God live in the kindness and joy of God's wing." Tony leaned over and whispered to her in an incredulous tone, "God has a wing?" To make matters worse, the cantor couldn't hit the notes. Francesca was shy about her own musical abilities and knew she was not an expert singer by any means, but her days in the choir enabled her to spot the man's off-key singing.

After Mass, there seemed to be a great hubbub at the back of the church. Parishioners were lined up to meet the new liturgist, and Francesca saw a few of them pumping his hand energetically. Others looked more restrained in their greeting. Francesca and Tony lined up to shake Father Bunt's hand as was the custom. As they waited, Francesca glanced at the liturgist. He was tall, solidly built, and had a beard, though not one of those long bushy ones she couldn't stand. *Early forties. Not bad looking at all.* She was not surprised to see a number of single female parishioners buzzing around him.

As she and Tony made their way toward the back door, Francesca stopped in front of one of the wall plaques illustrating the Stations of the Cross.

"That's strange," she said, eyes narrowing.

"What is?" Tony edged closer to the wall.

"Well, someone has changed the Stations! Instead of the pictures we used to have, you know, showing Jesus carrying the Cross on the way to Calvary . . ." Here words failed her.

"What the heck is a picture of a whale doing on the wall?" Tony asked in an incredulous tone.

She picked up a pamphlet from a stack below the stained-glass window. "I . . . I . . . can't believe this! Tony, this pamphlet says these are something called the 'Stations of the Earth.'"

"What in blazes is that?"

"Listen to this: in the twelfth station, where Jesus dies on the Cross, there's a prayer to Mother Earth. 'How do we pollute you, Mother Earth? Let us count the ways.'"

She handed him the pamphlet, and he quickly rifled through it.

"This can't be true," he said. "The second station has something about the . . . get this . . . the *web of creation*, and it mentions condo development and the plight of . . . the Pacific pocket mouse?!"

He looked at her mournfully. "Francesca, when I was a kid, the Stations were about Jesus suffering and dying. When did that change?"

"Tony, I have no idea. We've had the standard Stations for as long as I can remember. I can't believe Father Bunt would approve this stuff."

"Yeah, well, *somebody* did." Tony put the rumpled pamphlet back on the pile.

"Do you want to go for coffee?" He took her arm and was propelling her out the back of the church.

"Sure, but don't you want to meet the new guy?"

"Frankly, not right now. I think I need some time to digest all the changes."

They climbed into Tony's truck and headed to a Decatur coffee shop called Roasty Toasty. It was one of the many cafés where coffee was no longer described as "small," "medium," and "large" but rather with more exotic adjectives: in this case, "teeny-weeny," "tremendous," and "stupendous."

"I'll have a stupendous coffee of the day," said Francesca

"Give me a small," Tony said dryly. He had told her that he found the trendy coffee titles ridiculous and refused to use them.

As they were eating their bagels, he brought up the topic that was clearly bothering him.

"Francesca, I hate to say this, but Mass was more like a pep rally today. I'm starting to wonder if I'm too old-fashioned for Saint Rita's."

She felt her heart sink. She didn't want anything to discourage Tony's decision to return to his faith. *Lord, help me to say the right thing.*

"Tony, I'm sure things will settle down once the new guy gets used to the parish. He's probably just . . . well . . . a little too enthusiastic about his new job. I'm sure Father Bunt will tone him down."

Tony didn't look convinced. "Well, I hope so. You know Bunt better than I do." He sipped his coffee thoughtfully. "Look, Francesca, don't get the wrong idea. I'm not going to stop going to church just because the music is different and the Stations are . . . well, I guess 'updated' is one word. I mean, I have a pretty good grasp of what . . . I mean *Who* . . . is on the altar. That's why we go, right?"

She smiled, feeling a chill of tenderness running along her spine. "Yes, that's why we go."

* * * *

Father Bunt sat at his desk, sipping his cup of coffee and eating a biscuit. He and Father William had covered the morning Masses, and now he had a stretch of time before Maria served lunch. The music had been . . . *different* today; that was for sure. But he didn't think different was necessarily bad. The cantor was a new touch, but he knew many churches were now using them. The idea, as Chip had explained it, made sense. Many people wouldn't sing if they didn't have someone to follow.

Father Bunt didn't consider himself a traditionalist when it came to music. He thought some of the newer songs were fine, although he'd told Chip to also include the older hymns, since the parishioners were accustomed to them. Today it seemed Chip maybe had gone somewhat overboard with the modern folk tunes, but Father Bunt figured it would all get sorted out in time. Besides, it seemed like Chip knew his stuff when it came to music, and Father Bunt's own knowledge was limited—though even he had noticed that the cantor had been unable to hit the notes. *Heck, it was the man's first day; anyone would be nervous.*

He had noticed some of the parishioners making sour faces during the hymns, and he knew he'd probably be hearing complaints from the parish's self-anointed guardians of tradition. But he was tired of all the Vatican II debates. He just wanted to be a priest: say Mass, visit the sick, bury the dead, that sort of thing. He considered himself a middle-of-the-road guy. He didn't consider himself progressive by any means if that meant diluting Church teachings, but music was just window dressing. It didn't matter that much to him. He knew some parishioners from his previous parishes had nearly had heart attacks whenever contemporary music was played, but he rather liked its upbeat quality. In other ways he was more traditional. He liked to be called by his last name, for example, rather than "Father Brent." *Respect never goes out of style.*

He didn't want to micromanage the situation, so his plan was to have Chip handle the complaints. His hope was that, long term, the benefits of hiring a liturgist would outweigh the problems. If that didn't pan out, then the man would have to go. He hadn't hired Chip to make life even more troublesome than it already was.

Father Bunt stood up and went over to the window, where he noticed a squirrel sitting in the nook of a tree, staring back at him. He stood there for a few moments, enjoying the serenity of the bucolic scene: the well-trimmed green lawn, the finely shaped hedges. He had made sure that the lawn-service people understood that the church grounds had to be kept in shape. *First impressions are important.*

* * * *

Francesca looked up from her bagel and saw that the liturgist was in the café and headed straight for their table. He was beaming a big toothy smile and carrying a stupendous cup of coffee along with an order of Roasty Toasty, the restaurant's cheese toast. The man had a dog with him, a small black terrier with twisted little teeth that protruded from its mouth.

"Hey, don't you answer phones at the church?" He pulled out a chair at their table. "Mind if I join you?"

She noticed that Tony looked momentarily pained, but she replied, "Please do," and made the introductions.

"Ah, so this is the *paisano* table," Chip joked after hearing the last names. Then he looked at Tony and grinned.

"Oh, I see you have a teeny-weeny. I'm a stupendous man myself."

Tony took a big swallow of coffee and said nothing. Chip looked pleased with himself as he put cream in his coffee and bestowed another brilliant smile on them.

"Sit!" Chip suddenly gave a sharp tug on the leash, and the dog collapsed obediently at his feet, letting out a little snarl.

"I didn't know restaurants allowed dogs," Tony said.

"Oh, I just snuck him in. Besides, Wormwood here doesn't bite." Chip paused. "Unless you try to pet him, of course." Then he chuckled. "He has a special fondness for children."

Francesca noticed that the dog was staring at her with a steady, almost malevolent gaze. Chip tossed the dog a piece of toast, and there was a quick growling sound as he caught it.

Now Chip leaned in a bit closer to Tony and Francesca. "So what did you think of the changes at Mass today?"

"I, er, uh, well . . ." Francesca looked at Tony for help.

Tony drummed his fingers on the table. "Well, to tell you the truth, we were kind of surprised. That is, we didn't expect . . ."

But Chip cut him off. "I know what you mean. The parish has been stuck in the old ways for so long that it's going to take a while to adjust to the new."

He threw another crust to Wormwood. "But I've seen this before in other parishes; invariably, folks come around and they wonder how they ever wanted the other stuff."

"The other stuff?" Tony's voice had an icy edge.

"You know—the organ, the chant, the Latin." He shuddered. "All that pre–Vatican II garbage."

A dangerous flush was spreading over Tony's features, and Francesca feared what he might say next, so she decided to change the subject.

"Tell us something about yourself, Chip. Where are you from?"

She soon regretted her impulse, for Chip launched into a detailed rundown of his life and résumé that lasted nearly half an hour. He also revealed what he called his "vision" for the parish. He said he really wanted to "get the spirit moving" by offering teen Masses, more "upbeat" music, cantors at every Mass, and maybe some liturgical dances for important occasions like Holy Week and Easter.

"Holy Week? Dances?" Francesca repeated the words in disbelief.

"Well, something subtle, you know, to get a more positive and cheerful feel to the occasion. Something that shows we're really an Easter People. Take Holy Thursday: we could have a dance that symbolizes washing feet."

"Symbolizes it? But we actually do it—the washing, I mean."

The look he gave her made her feel momentarily as if she were a member of a primitive tribe that worshipped trees.

"You just wait—the dances transform what has been a rather dry . . . well, you know . . ."—here he dropped his volume as if discussing an embarrassing medical condition—"ritual. Instead, we'll have something with a contemporary feel . . . something the young people will really love."

"You mean like hip-hop?" Tony's voice had a controlled tone to it that Francesca hadn't heard before. *He's really steamed.*

"Well, sure, they use that in some parishes, and the kids really get into it. You see, the way I look at it, the Church has to reach kids where they are, you know, give them something that really moves them. For some kids, it's hard rock, but for others, well, hip-hop is just the thing."

Tony gripped his coffee cup tightly. "So there's no difference really between a rock festival and a church service?"

Chip blinked rapidly. "Sure there is. But even in church, young people don't want this 'Holy God We Praise Thy Name' stuff."

Chip wiped his fingers carefully on a napkin. "Look, let's face it: there's all kinds of things competing for kids' attention these days. The Church has got to stay in the running, you know, attract the crowds."

Tony picked up a plastic knife and turned it over. "So just give them what they want, right?"

Chip seemed to miss the sarcastic tone. "*Exactly. You* know what I'm talking about. The Church has to keep moving and progressing—keep up with the times."

"Kind of like a shark you mean? You know—if they stop moving, they die."

Chip chuckled. "I like that. Mind if I use it sometime?"

Tony started to reply, but Chip suddenly looked at his watch and stood up. "Oh, gosh, I'd love to talk more. This has been so interesting, but I have to go meet Father Bunt." He paused and chuckled.

"I keep calling him Father Brent, but he prefers Bunt. I guess he thinks the old-fashioned way sounds better."

And with that comment, he yanked on the dog's leash and hurried away. As they made their way out of the restaurant and onto the sidewalk, Francesca saw a small child reaching out to pet the dog and then saw him pull back his hand and scream.

Francesca turned to Tony. "Well, I guess it's pretty obvious who orchestrated the all-new Stations of the Earth."

Tony nodded. "I'm sure the Pacific pocket mouse will thank him for it."

Chapter 4

I'm not going to finish the pistachio ice cream in the freezer. I don't need another treat today.

Francesca was a card-holding member of the Quart Club at Bruster's, the little ice cream store on Lawrenceville Highway, which offered customers a free, hand-packed quart after they bought six. At the store there was a very friendly Pakistani lady who appreciated Francesca's frequent visits and always packed the containers extra full just for her. Now Francesca debated with herself as she contemplated the luscious treat that seemed to be calling her name.

If I finish it all, the temptation will be gone, and I can start a whole new diet tomorrow.

But another voice chimed in: *Wouldn't it be better to start the diet now and keep the ice cream as a treat for next weekend?*

The two voices continued bringing up points and counterpoints until she rose in exasperation from the couch and headed for the refrigerator. But just as she was opening the freezer door, the phone rang. She usually let the machine answer, picking up only if she knew the caller. The voicemail recording had her asking callers to "leave a message with Tubs the cat," followed by the sound of the old cat purring loudly. Now she was surprised to hear Chip Cambio on the line. Curious, she picked up the phone. "Hello?"

"I hope I'm not speaking out of turn, Francesca, but I wondered if you might like to have supper with me one night. I'd like to get to know some of the choir crowd better, and I understand you're an alto."

She hesitated. *Does he mean this to be a date?* She and Tony were not engaged, and they had never promised one another to give up dating other people. Still, she had the impression that Tony was not going out with anyone but her.

"Francesca, are you still there?"

Curiosity got the best of her. Having supper with Chip would provide more detailed insights into his plans to change the parish. Maybe she could influence him to back off a bit.

"Oh, sorry—I just had to look at my calendar. How about, uh, two weeks from today?"

"Well, you must be one popular lady if I have to wait that long!"

"Uh, er . . . ," she stuttered, but he broke in.

"Just kidding. I'll put it on the calendar and look forward to it! Ciao."

After hanging up, Francesca made a beeline for the freezer and dished herself out a generous portion of ice cream, remembering to put a dollop in Tubs's bowl. She knew the old fellow also liked a treat now and again. Then she marked the date on her calendar. *Now what have I done? I have no desire to go out with that man.*

* * * *

Father William was in his room down the hall from Father Bunt's, working on his sermon for the following Sunday. *I want to talk about Pope Benedict XVI always receiving the Host on his tongue and always while kneeling. There is a proper, reverent way to approach the Eucharist.* His fingers paused at the keyboard as he recalled two teenagers wandering up to Communion in flip-flops and old T-shirts. He had also spotted someone chewing gum. *But do I dare bring up this topic now that things are changing so much at Saint Rita's?*

Last Sunday, the cantor had sung a contemporary version of the "Agnus Dei," partly in English and partly in Latin. Unfortunately, he had botched the Latin, mispronouncing *agnus* as "Agnes." Afterward, a few parishioners had jokingly asked Father William whether Agnes Day was a new Saint. Then there were all these hymns with feel-good words that seemed more suited to a children's TV show than the Holy Mass. He had heard one parishioner sum up "Shepherd Me, Oh God" as exuding "marshmallowy goodness."

But what really disturbed him was the way the new liturgist had apparently assumed responsibility over him, the assistant pastor. It seemed that memos related to the liturgy—which in Father John's day were issued by the pastor—were now coming from Cambio. One had really upset Father William, stating in no uncertain terms that there would no longer be any silence during and after Communion.

People would be singing a hymn as they approached the altar, and another hymn would immediately follow that, which meant there would be no time for quiet prayer. When Father William had tried to talk with Father Bunt about the memo, Father Bunt had waved him off, explaining Cambio was making those kinds of decisions. It looked like the new chain of command was pastor, liturgist, and then assistant pastor.

Father William paced his room, deep in thought. He wandered over to see how Ignatius was doing. He poked around a bit in the mountain of litter, expecting a nose to emerge. Then he dug more intently. And then he froze.

The cage was empty.

* * * *

Down the hall, Father Bunt was at his desk, sipping a mug of steaming coffee. He was still trying to get used to the rumbling of the subway trains, which occasionally awakened him at night. Sometimes the noise became incorporated into his dreams. Last night, he had dreamt he was wearing armor and battling a dragon that was living in an underground cave. *No wonder I'm tired.*

He yawned as he contemplated his job. It seemed there was an endless amount of paperwork to attend to, plus a constant stream of events that he was expected to show up for. His spirits sank as he looked at the list of phone calls that had come in while he had been at a Knights of Columbus luncheon. It looked like there were plenty of parishioners who wanted to talk to him—and not the new liturgist—about the changes in the Mass. But he was determined not to spend time on this issue; that's why he had hired Chip in the first place. *Just let him do his job and we can reevaluate in six months or so.*

Just then, he spotted something moving in the corner of his office. It was small and fuzzy and scampering at a fast clip. *Mice! Just what we need here at the zoo.*

He picked up the phone and dialed Maria's extension to let her know. But he certainly hadn't expected her reaction. As soon as she heard the word "mouse," she let out a blood-curdling scream as he heard a crashing sound downstairs in the kitchen. *There goes lunch.*

* * * *

Francesca was readying the house to host a meeting of the Choir Chicks. As she ran the vacuum in the living room, she wondered if she'd have to change the group's name. Currently, the women who came to these gatherings were in the choir, but with the music changing, would they all stay? Would she?

A few hours later, the doorbell rang, and the women started coming in. First it was Shirley Evans, carrying a bottle of chilled Chardonnay and a plate of brownies. Francesca often imagined Shirley with wings, perhaps because she looked like a Christmas-card cherub with her round, rosy-cheeked face, auburn curls, and little upturned nose. Shirley was in her midtwenties, married, and the mother of a two-year-old girl, Gracie. Francesca suspected Shirley wouldn't be happy about the changes at church, since she had heard her say numerous times that she wanted Gracie to know the same traditions that she did.

Next came Rebecca with a bottle of Merlot and a low-fat quiche. Francesca accepted the quiche with a smile, although she feared it would be inedible. Her well-meaning friend was always trying the latest in dietetic recipes, which she claimed tasted "real," although Francesca secretly disagreed. The last in was Molly Flowers, brandishing a small potted plant, which she called her obligatory hostess gift. As she was fond of saying, this was a tradition no Southern woman would ever do away with. She also had a fruit-and-cheese tray, plus a tin of homemade cookies.

Molly, a nurse in labor and delivery at DeKalb Medical Center, had a syrupy Southern drawl, hinting at her roots in Destin, Florida, part of the Redneck Riviera. Although she was quick to point out that a lady never revealed her age, she had once confided to the group that she was "pushing 50." Her hair was raven black and short, and her green eyes were expertly made up. She was a self-proclaimed feminist who sometimes annoyed the other Choir Chicks with her opinions, but she was also the kind of person who would do anything to help a friend.

The women arranged the food upon the coffee table in the living room, while Francesca opened the first bottle of wine. She had a feeling the Choir Chicks were eager to analyze the latest situation in the parish.

"What do you think about greeting each other before Mass?" Rebecca asked, as the women were filling their dishes with food.

Molly grimaced. "Sugar, if you ask me, it's worse than holding hands during the Our Father. For Heaven's sake, why do we need to shake hands at the beginning of Mass? It reminds me of the nursing conventions I go to."

Francesca took a sip of wine. That was her exact opinion, but she wanted to see how the others felt before joining in. She was starting to feel nervous because at some point she would have to tell the group she had accepted Chip's dinner invitation. She didn't want them to think she was consorting with the enemy.

"Well, since it happens before Mass actually starts, I guess it isn't liturgically wrong," Shirley noted. "But it still bugs me. It just feels . . . well . . . dumb."

Rebecca nodded. "And what about the hymns? I mean, some of the lyrics sound like nursery school or something."

Shirley reached for a cookie. "Yeah, it reminds me of the Barney music that Gracie likes. Plus we're always singing about ourselves. I actually sat down and studied the lyrics—and in one hymn, the words 'God' and 'Jesus' never show up—but I counted 'we' and 'us' 23 times!"

Molly put down her wine glass. "Well, some of the new music I actually like. It's kind of cheery, you know. But that whatchamacallit hymn about body parts really bugs me, and I came up with my own words for it." She paused until she was sure she had everyone's attention, then crooned, "And your big derriere that gets caught in the chair causes people to stare . . ."

After the laughter died down, Rebecca posed a question. "What do you think about the new guy? The liturgist? I think he's rather handsome, although . . ."

But just then the doorbell rang.

"Are you expecting anyone else?" Molly wanted to know.

"No, not at all." Francesca peeked through the peephole and spotted someone she had not expected to see on her front porch for a few weeks. It was Chip Cambio. *Did he get the day wrong?*

She opened the door. "Chip! What a pleasant surprise!" She could feel her face reddening from the lie.

He bustled in, carrying a bottle of white Zinfandel and a large bag with the Roasty Toasty emblem—a clown brandishing a coffee cup the size of a garbage can and wearing a huge bagel on his head.

"Good evening, ladies! I heard through the grapevine about the Choir Chicks, and I figured this would be a good way to get to know you better. I hope you don't mind my showing up unannounced."

Without waiting for an answer, he sat down in a nearby chair, placed the bottle of wine on the table, and opened the bag.

"Fresh-baked apple pie from Roasty Toasty."

Francesca quickly introduced the women to Chip, who stood up and politely shook their outstretched hands. He then sat down again and began filling his plate with food, nodding when Francesca offered him a glass of wine.

"Thank you. What a wonderful spread." Then, once he had cut a big slice of the pie for himself, he went on: "Ladies, don't let me interrupt. You continue with your discussion, and I'll just sit back and listen."

Shirley was the first one to regain her composure. "Well, Chip, we were talking about the changes at Saint Rita's. And I hope this won't be a big shock to you"—here she paused for a sip of wine—"but not everyone is exactly loving them so far."

Chip chewed his food with a thoughtful expression on his face. "You mean the music?"

"Well, for starters, yes."

"Look, people come to church after a long week," Chip said. "The boss yells at them, they go home, and the kids are screaming. They have overdue bills. You know, a real mess. So they come to church and they want . . . well, they want to feel better. To be uplifted, you see. And that's what I'm trying to do."

Francesca decided to jump in. "So it's all about making people feel good?"

"Not just that, but, yeah, what's wrong with religion giving people some relief?"

"But Chip, for Heaven's sake," Shirley said, "you make Mass sound like an anesthetic or something."

He grimaced. "Well, that's somewhat extreme, obviously, but if you don't leave Mass feeling better than when you showed up, why come back?"

"How about the Sacraments?" Shirley said quietly.

"Oh, sure, them." He brushed a tiny flake of pie crust off his leg.

Francesca couldn't resist asking one more question. "Chip, how do the new . . . uh . . . Stations of the Earth fit in with your . . . er . . . vision?"

Now Chip looked excited. "Oh, you saw those, huh? See, the point is to link the Stations with contemporary issues, make them relevant for people today. This year it's the environment, and another year we'll do other issues, you know, like gender equality, social justice, the whole nine yards."

Molly looked pleased. "I think it's about time Saint Rita's did something about women's issues."

Chip nodded. "Believe me, these Stations really speak to people. You'd be amazed at how popular they were at my last church."

Francesca was relieved when Shirley took up the gauntlet, her growing annoyance and two glasses of Chardonnay giving an edge to her voice: "Just because something's *popular* doesn't make it *right*, Chip!"

Chip grinned and held his hands up in a mock gesture of surrender. "Ladies, hold your fire! Give the new guy a chance!"

Then he shrugged again and shook his head, still smiling. "Look, I'm not a philosopher. I just know what works."

With that, he made a big show of taking a small notebook from his shirt pocket and opening it. Meanwhile, Francesca was desperately trying to figure out if there might be a way to salvage the evening. But she realized they were stuck with Chip's company. She simply didn't have the heart to hurt his feelings, no matter how obtuse he might be. She sighed and opened another bottle of wine.

"Well, we could talk about this stuff until the cows come home," he said. "But right now, I need some cantors to lead the Sunday Masses, and I've heard there are some good, strong voices in this room."

Darting a glance at Rebecca, the lead alto, Francesca noticed that her friend was avoiding her eyes. She suspected that Rebecca would not want to be a cantor, but she wasn't sure how her friend could graciously refuse. From that point on, the meeting of the Choir Chicks became Chip's show. He managed to get both Rebecca and Shirley to sign the cantor sheet, then spent the rest of the time talking about himself: his childhood in Florida, his years as an altar boy, and the time he'd spent in seminary.

Even Molly, who usually didn't hesitate to speak her mind, couldn't seem to get a word in edgewise. Instead, she sat quietly, downing glass after glass of wine. When the grandfather clock in the living room struck 11, the group began to break up. Much to Francesca's dismay, however, after the women had all left, Chip remained in her living room.

He seemed completely at home as he poured them each another glass of wine. Then he left his chair and took a seat next to Francesca on the couch. Despite his forward behavior and wretched theology, there *was* something attractive about him, she thought. He was meticulously well groomed and his clothes looked finely tailored. He spoke with an easy manner that projected a winning confidence. Just as she was turning these thoughts over in her mind, something happened that later made her realize how much she'd had to drink. Chip startled her by leaning close and gently grasping her hand, then turning it over and brushing his lips against the palm. She was very surprised to discover he had found a new erogenous zone. She was even more surprised that she wasn't stopping him.

What now? she thought desperately—and the doorbell rang.

"Saved by the bell?" His voice was husky.

She jumped up and squinted through the little opening in the door, and her heart sank. It was Tony. When she opened the door, he explained that he had been in the neighborhood and had seen her light on. He decided to stop by to say hello. Then he glanced into the living room and she knew what he was seeing: empty wine bottles, the remnants of the cheese and fruit tray—and, of course, Chip seated comfortably on the couch.

Chip grinned. "Good to see you again, Tony!"

Tony looked grim. "Same here." Then he turned to Francesca. "I didn't realize you had company. I'll call you tomorrow."

And with that, he was gone.

Chapter 5

Maria entered the kitchen at Saint Rita's as if she were walking across a minefield. Ever since childhood, she'd had a phobia about mice. And ever since Father Bunt had told her about the mouse in his office, she had taken every shadow and every little sound as evidence that Saint Rita's was infiltrated with rodents of all shapes and sizes. She nervously began mixing flour and shortening for the pie crust, certain that any moment she would reach for the sugar or salt and confront a mouse.

The door to the kitchen opened and she jumped, nearly overturning her cup of coffee. She turned to see Chip walking in carrying a big cluster of red roses.

"I thought you'd like these to brighten up the kitchen a bit." He gave a little bow and then handed her the bouquet.

"Oh, they're gorgeous. Thank you!" She inhaled the delicious scent.

"How's everything going?" He eyed the pie pan. "What's for lunch?"

She glanced at her watch. It was only 8 a.m., and she wouldn't have lunch on the table until noon. Normally, she only served the priests lunch, but it looked like Chip was inviting himself.

"We're having fried catfish, greens, squash casserole, baby carrots . . ." Her voice trailed off as she realized that Chip was staring at her.

"Mmmmm, that all sounds marvelous."

Suddenly he moved so close to her that she could see a small, half-moon-shaped scar on his forehead that she'd never noticed before.

"You know, you're a really beautiful lady. But I'll bet you hear that all the time, right?"

Flustered, she didn't know what to do. She was, after all, a married woman with a family. Still, he seemed to be joking, and she didn't want to overreact. Just as she was trying to put some distance between the two of them, the kitchen door opened again. This time it was Father William.

She could see the young priest drawing a quick, obvious conclusion, which brought blood to his cheeks. As Maria backed far away from Chip, she was sure she was also blushing furiously.

"Father William, can I get you a cup of coffee or something?"

The young priest was looking down at the floor, as if to avoid her eyes. Then, suddenly the expression on his face turned to one of pure delight.

"I think I've just spotted Ignatius! It's not a mouse that's loose in the rectory—it's my hamster!"

The whole situation had strained her to the breaking point. At the sound of the word "mouse," Maria fell to the floor in a dead faint.

* * * *

Francesca decided to stop by the day chapel at Saint Rita's to spend an hour in silent prayer. She thought dismally about the night before. She had managed to get Chip to leave by claiming she was getting a headache. She knew that was the oldest excuse in the world, but she had been desperate, and it had worked. She had hoped that Tony might call when he got home, but the phone had remained stubbornly silent. Rather morosely, she had climbed into bed with Tubs.

She had not slept very well, however, and at daybreak when she heard the catbirds screeching in her front yard, she decided she needed some prayer time. Fortunately, the chapel was open 24/7 for parishioners who wanted to be in the presence of the Lord. One of Francesca's favorite devotions was praying there in silence because at home there were so many distractions.

But the moment she walked into the chapel, she knew everything had changed. Someone—Chip?—had added speakers in the corners, and there was some trite, cloying tune filling every corner of the chapel like smoke from a toxic-waste dump. She saw Sister Therese, the principal of Saint Rita's school, sitting in the back row. Francesca took a pew up front and knelt down, trying to ignore the music. But the lyrics, which had something to do with a "cup of hope," were so distracting that she found it impossible to pray.

As she stood up to leave the chapel, she turned around and saw Sister Therese hurrying out too. Francesca only knew Sister from short conversations in the rectory. She was about five foot eight and wiry with pale-blue eyes that were slightly magnified by her bifocals. Her skin was smooth, giving her the appearance of being much younger than her age, which Francesca judged to be midfifties.

According to Rebecca, Sister Therese had led an "interesting" life before becoming a nun. She had been previously married to a man prone to physical and verbal abuse, and after finally divorcing him, she'd found a new life in Christ, eventually entering the convent. But that was only about five years before, and in Rebecca's opinion, Sister Therese had never completely lost what Rebecca called "street smarts." This made her a valued counselor for troubled parishioners—as Rebecca had put it, "You can really *talk* to her; she understands real life, you know, relationship troubles, credit card debt, kids on drugs." But, as Francesca had heard through the grapevine, it also left some in fear of Sister's unpredictable temper.

Sister Therese was waiting for Francesca outside the chapel. "Have you ever in your life seen, or I should say, *heard* such nonsense?" Sister's veil trembled with every word. "It's a travesty, a sacrilege, an utter . . ." Here, Sister's words seemed to die out, as if she had written the last check on her vocabulary bank.

"You mean the . . . uh . . . music, Sister?"

"Indeed I do. And it's not just that—but the changes at Mass—the blasted . . . whatdoyoucallem . . . cantors, the rinky-dink piano music, the dumbed-down lyrics . . ." Here she paused and took a deep breath.

"I just don't understand how one man can have the amount of control that . . . that . . . blasted *liturgist* has in this parish. If you ask me, somebody should do *some*thing to rein him in, and soon!" And with that comment, Sister Therese hurried out of the church.

* * * *

It was the first choir practice with the new director. Francesca had heard rumors that the man had been hired by Chip, and although she had serious misgivings about the direction the music would be taking, she decided to show up for rehearsal anyway.

As she took her usual place in the choir area, she was relieved to see many familiar faces: Rebecca, Shirley, and Molly were all there, along with Bertha Chumley, the stocky alto who wore dresses big enough to conceal a small village. She also saw Andy Dull, a well-intentioned man who rarely hit the right notes but at least lacked volume. Gavin Stewart, a decent tenor, was also there, plus others who had been in the choir many years.

She was, however, startled to see quite a few new faces. Then she remembered that Chip had inserted a notice in the bulletin urging parishioners to join the choir and "lift up your voices in praise and worship." The blurb had assured readers that even if they weren't good singers, there would still be a place for them in the choir. That kind of anything-goes attitude had infuriated the last choir director. She recalled him saying, "No one wants a volunteer brain surgeon in the operating room. Why assume that when it comes to singing, anyone can do it?"

The new director was sitting behind the piano, rummaging through a stack of music. He looked to be in his fifties, very thin and hunched over, and with a head that was completely bald except for six or seven coal-black strands neatly arranged across the top. Rebecca nudged her and whispered, "Now *that's* a comb-over."

Francesca was not at all surprised to see that Chip was also there, looking confident and upbeat, beaming a radiant smile at every person who walked in.

"Great to see everyone," Chip enthused. "Come on in and pick up a packet of music and a book."

Francesca's heart sank when she saw that the book in question was the volume called *Breaking Bread.*

"What happened to the red books?" Andy Dull called out from behind her.

The choir director looked confused, but Chip had the answer.

"Oh, you must mean *Worship II*. Well, we sent those out to have their, uh, their bindings fixed. Many of them were quite old and needed some repairs."

"So they'll be back once they're fixed?" someone else asked.

Chip adjusted his tie. "Yes, that's correct."

Molly was sitting behind Francesca, and leaned forward to whisper in her ear. "He probably burned them."

The first hymn they went over had the familiar melody of "Come, Thou Font of Every Blessing," but the lyrics were about "singing a new church into being." One of the tenors lost it after they had gone through the first verse. "Why do we need a new church? What's wrong with the old one?" And before there could be further discussion, the man packed up his music and left.

Other longtime members of the choir appeared disgruntled, and afterward, when a small crowd gathered on the front steps of the church, Francesca noticed that even the usually placid Andy Dull sounded angry, and Bertha, who tended to keep her opinions to herself, was chiming in about how bad things were. A number of people said they would not be returning to the choir, and Francesca realized at that moment that she was among them. Her heart was no longer in it.

* * * *

Father Bunt looked dismally at his to-do list for the day. He didn't mind going to see the old folks at the Eternal Sunrise nursing home, nor did he mind hearing confessions, celebrating daily Mass, attending the monthly church supper, conferring with parishioners about upcoming events, and overseeing the parish council meeting. But what was really getting on his nerves was the amount of time he was now spending defending the liturgist. The man had only been in the parish a short time, but he'd already made enormous changes. The plan had been to give Cambio free rein for six months, and Father Bunt was determined to stick to that decision, but meanwhile it seemed that every time he turned around there was someone wanting to fill his ear with complaints. Even when he told people to talk directly to Cambio, they just didn't seem to get it.

There was a knock on the door. In stepped Mrs. Alma Reedley, head of the Golden Glories club at Saint Rita's, where once a month people over 60 gathered for lunches and socializing. She was a plump woman with tightly permed grey hair and a round face wreathed in wrinkles. She had been at the parish over 40 years, and Father Bunt knew she was well loved. But today she looked distressed.

"Father, I really am not one to complain, you know that. But Chip Cambio, bless his heart, well, I just don't know how to say this."

"Mrs. Reedley, please have a seat. Now, what seems to be the problem?"

"Well, Father, Chip came to a Golden Glories meeting. We were delighted, of course, since we like to welcome newcomers to the parish. But Father, he . . ." She twisted her wedding ring nervously. "Well, Father, he seemed to just take over the meeting."

"How do you mean?" *Please, dear God, let her be brief and to the point.*

"Well, he tried to get our members to sign up to be lectors. Father, you know as well as I do that not everyone is cut out to do the readings. But he made it sound like it didn't matter if someone had a good speaking voice or not."

"Well, I'm sure he's just trying to be . . . uh . . . encouraging, that's all."

"I'm sure that's it, Father." Mrs. Reedley's facial expression belied her words. "But he treated us as if we were children or something." She hesitated and then clutched the small crucifix that rested on her ample bosom.

"Bless his heart, Father, he said that anyone who signed up to become a lector would get a deck of playing cards with the Saints on them!"

Father Bunt cleared his throat nervously. "Well, that is a bit . . . uh, did anyone actually sign up?"

Mrs. Reedley let out a large sigh. "Yes, Father, unfortunately, Horace Green and Pamela Spruill did."

He looked at her expectantly. "Is there a problem then?"

"Father, they both mumble when they speak. And Pamela is terrified of standing at a podium. Chip told her that reading at Mass was a great way to get her over her fears!"

He cleared his throat and straightened some papers on his desk.

"Father, that's not all. When some members asked him why he was changing the music, he got a little angry. Art Bruner pointed out that the pope himself likes Gregorian chant and classical music at Mass . . ." She continued to fiddle with her ring.

"Yes, Mrs. Reedley, please go on."

"Chip said the pope was too old to know what was what."

Father Bunt removed his reading glasses and fished in his pocket for a handkerchief to clean them with. It was a habit he used to stall for time, one that had supplanted the whole ritual of smoking cigarettes, given up years ago.

"Well, Mrs. Reedley, thank you for coming by. I will be sure to take care of this matter."

"I knew you would understand, Father. Thank you so much."

After she left, he didn't have another moment to think. The phones rang all morning. He heard from people who were upset because music was being piped in to the adoration chapel. Others were disgruntled about being told to greet their neighbors in the pews before Mass began. One man blasted the changes in the Stations of the Cross: "Father, if I want to worship nature, I can go to the Existentialist church across town!"

He looked at a little index card on his desk, where he was keeping score of the number of times he had heard the exact same joke: "Do you know the difference between a liturgist and a terrorist?" By now he was well aware of the punch line, but he let the parishioners deliver it: "You can reason with a terrorist." The tally for the joke now stood at 20, but he had long since stopped laughing.

Some people were threatening to leave the parish, while others were digging in their heels and insisting the pastor take charge. But there were some who favored what Chip was doing, although Father Bunt was nervous about their praise. One lady told Father Bunt how much she and her friends approved of the new "Stations of the Earth," but she was the same woman who the previous year had staged a protest after Father John refused to wash her dog's paws on Holy Thursday. Father Bunt shuddered to think what might happen during Holy Week next year.

He toyed with a pencil. *I'd better go take a look at those new Stations, and fast.* One thing was for sure: if the complaints got out of hand—or if collections plummeted—he would be in hot water with the archbishop.

I guess I should have a short meeting with Chip. That wouldn't be micromanaging; it would be more like putting out a fire before it spreads. He dialed the extension to the liturgist's office. When he got voice mail, he hung up. *I'll see him in person.* Just then, Father Bunt heard a scratching sound outside his office door. He had heard that the hamster was loose in the rectory, but this sounded like a much bigger animal. *Maybe the thing has somehow quadrupled in size. Nothing would surprise me that much in this place.*

He threw open the door and stared down at a very large, extremely unkempt, yellowish-white, poodle-type dog with a big eager tongue lolling from its open mouth and a small pool of drool forming by its crooked front paws. The pungent dog seemed to be in need of a bath and a trim, and its toenails were so long they had clawed ridges in the bottom of Father Bunt's door.

"Maria!" He called downstairs, and he heard the sounds of footsteps on the stairs.

"Yes, Father. What do you want?"

And then she spied the dog. "Oh, you've met the new dog! Isn't he just the cutest thing? He showed up yesterday at the kitchen door. He's a stray, bless his heart."

"I'm not sure we have room for a dog in the rectory." Father Bunt chose his words carefully, for he knew Maria was a big animal lover. He had also heard rumors about how temperamental Maria could be, and he didn't want to cross her. He pictured in his mind's eye a luscious, flaky blueberry pie with wings, flying through an open window in the rectory kitchen and disappearing into the sky.

"Oh, Father, he is just the sweetest thang." Her Southern accent was thickening. "Of course, he's a little, uh, slow, aren't you, darlin'?"

She bent down to pet the animal, and the dog's response was to throw himself on his back so she could reach his shaggy stomach.

Father relented. "Well, OK . . . I suppose we can keep it if it stays downstairs." He hesitated. "Does it . . . he . . . have a name?"

"Yes, he does, Father. The children have already named him!"

He waited hopefully. He liked animals to respond to standard titles like Rover, Whitey, or Rex.

"They've named him Dopey."

He repeated the name with a question mark at the end, hoping he had heard it wrong, but Maria assured him that he had it right.

"You see, he's not too good with commands just yet, but I know he'll learn. And one of the first graders called him 'Dopey' and he answered right away."

"Dopey," she said loudly. "Sit! Sit! *Sit*!

The dog stood on all four paws and gazed at her. Father Bunt noted that the expression remained the same: tongue lolling out and ears perked up. The drooling continued unabated.

"It's like pushing a rope, Father. But we're fixin' to work on that, aren't we, Dopey?"

Undaunted, she took a small stick out of her apron pocket and threw it gently down the hall. "Fetch it, Dopey! Go get it, boy!"

The dog sat down.

* * * *

Francesca didn't know what to do about Tony. Ever since he had stopped by after the Choir Chicks' meeting and spotted Chip on the couch, he had not called her or come by again. She had tried calling him at home once or twice but only reached his answering machine, and she decided not to leave a message. She had seen him at Mass, and he had greeted her politely. But after Mass, he'd said he had to report to the office, so they hadn't gone out for coffee. What could she say? She was afraid that any explanation would only increase her guilt in his eyes.

Besides, she was a bit disturbed by his behavior. She didn't like how he had so quickly jumped to conclusions and condemned her without giving her a chance to explain. Then she remembered him once telling her that working in homicide had made him mistrustful of people and made it difficult to keep relationships with women going. She hadn't quite understood him at the time, but now she was beginning to see what he meant. She decided to give him more time. Surely he would come to his senses and realize the situation had been harmless.

But what if she told him that she had accepted a dinner invitation with Chip? Would that seem harmless as well? Francesca sighed loudly, and Tubs began purring, as if trying to reassure her that everything would be fine. She was tempted to break the date with Chip, who just seemed so incredibly self-centered. But how else could she find out his secret plans for the parish?

Another thought came to her. She was quite happy dating Tony and didn't want to spoil what they had. Then came a little voice in her head: *Yes, but you also know it is dangerous to assume that your relationship with Tony is serious. You have no way of knowing if he is dating other women, correct?*

Correct, she answered.

And you're doing nothing wrong, right?

Right, she replied.

She looked at the clock. If the internal dialogue went on much longer, Chip would be at her front door and she'd still be standing in her bedroom, attired in her leopard-print dressing gown and fuzzy pig slippers. *Time to get focused!* She selected an outfit with great care, reciting in her mind the requirements: nothing daring, low cut, suggestive, or fancy. *Gee, I wish I had a nun's habit; that would be perfect.*

She decided on a white cotton pullover and a black straight skirt that rested just at the knee. She wore her hair up, and not a trace of makeup. But then, when the doorbell rang, she quickly changed her mind, raced back into the bathroom, and added a quick touch of blush and some lipstick. *It's not that I want to attract him, but I also don't want to scare him away.*

Chip swept into the living room carrying a bottle of chilled champagne, a box of Italian chocolates, a cluster of bright yellow roses—and a little bag of cat treats for Tubs. He explained that the champagne would be for later, after supper, if that was all right with her. She was so mesmerized by the chocolates and so touched by the gift for Tubs that she just nodded her approval. She opened the little bag and gave a few of the treats to Tubs, and he devoured them in seconds. The old cat then began an elaborate washing-up routine, indicating his approval of the cuisine.

She had to admit that Chip looked remarkably handsome. His brown hair was gleaming and his beard was carefully trimmed. He was wearing another fine-looking suit with a silk tie, and she caught a whiff of that tempting cologne she had noticed before. He looked her up and down as if she were modeling the very latest in French fashions and declared she looked "gorgeous." Then he offered her his arm and escorted her to his car. It was a late-model Volvo and was spanking clean. There were leather seats and a fine sound system, which began playing, of all things, Gregorian chant.

She adjusted her seat belt carefully and caught his eye. "Interesting musical selection."

But the expression on his face was one of disdain. He roughly yanked the CD out of the player.

"I didn't realize that was in there. I loaned my car to my . . . er . . . friend the other night. His car was in the shop. He likes that stuff."

"And you?" She couldn't resist asking.

He threw the CD over his shoulder into the back seat as if it were a piece of trash. "I can't stand it. All that mumbo jumbo. It's like the Dark Ages or something."

She decided to keep quiet. There was no need to tell him how much she loved Gregorian chant. As they headed toward downtown Decatur, they passed the occasional car with windows rolled up and rap music playing so loudly inside that the asphalt seemed to shudder. She chuckled as she thought about the contrast between the two types of music.

"Wouldn't it be something if some day 'gangsta rap' music were playing at Mass?"

By the expression on his face, she realized the joke had fallen flat. He obviously did not find that possibility as outrageous as she did.

* * * *

Tony was at home. It was his day off and he had spent it doing yard work, going grocery shopping, changing the oil in his truck, and backing up his computer. He was trying to keep busy because there was something grating at the back of his mind: a nagging worry that would go away when he confronted it, but as soon as he got involved in something else it would start up again. He had made a vow to himself, after his last relationship had gone south, that he would never, ever, under any circumstances let another woman get under his skin. And then, of course, along came Francesca, and he had made a complete ass of himself.

He kept replaying that awkward scene in his mind. The way he had bounded up to her front porch, hoping to invite her out for a late-night drink, and then the embarrassment of seeing her there with Chip. *Of all people! That guy is such a buffoon; I thought Francesca would have better taste.*

He regretted the way he had reacted, storming off into the night, and he was sure that Chip had made some joke, and they had laughed at him together. He angrily ran his fingers through his hair. This was ridiculous. He should just call her and see what the explanation was. Maybe that guy Chip had shown up unannounced and refused to leave. That was probably it. He went to the phone and dialed her number, but he got the answering machine.

"Hey, it's Tony." But she didn't pick up.

Realizing he was hungry, he decided to go for some takeout. He would come back, open a cold beer, and eat the meal on his back deck. Then he would try her number later and maybe they could go out for dessert. He jumped into his well-worn Ford pickup, noting that it needed washing, and headed toward downtown Decatur.

Moments later, he pulled up in front of Benedetti's, the restaurant where he had taken Francesca on their first date, and he couldn't believe what he saw. There, emerging from a gleaming new car was none other than Francesca, who was being helped out by . . . and this he really couldn't believe . . . that Chip Cambio clown! Disgusted, Tony decided to forget about takeout. He would go home, throw a frozen meal into the microwave, and figure out what to do next. It looked like this situation between Chip and Francesca was picking up some steam.

Chapter 6

Father William had consulted one of his hamster books to find a way to lure Ignatius back to his cage. The book detailed a trap involving a small pail, litter, treats, and a few books. The litter provided cushioning at the bottom of the pail, where Father William placed some raisins and shelled nuts. A few books stacked by the pail would give the hamster a stairway leading to the top. Lured by the aroma of treats, the little fellow would then jump inside and be trapped.

Father William at first wasn't sure where to put the trap, but decided finally that a corner of the kitchen would work best. After all, he had last seen Ignatius there, and he reasoned that the hamster was probably snacking on bread crumbs and other tidbits that fell to the kitchen floor. He knew Maria was afraid of mice—and anything fast moving and furry in the rodent family—but he felt confident Ignatius would not scare her. After all, he was a very placid animal with light brown fur and two fuzzy tufts that stuck out cheerfully on either side of his rump. He had sharp teeth but was quite gentle. He had never bitten anyone.

Father William decided he would tell Maria about the trap first thing in the morning. If she really protested, he would, of course, move it. However, he was sure that Ignatius would be captured during the night, and the whole problem would be resolved shortly.

Humming a few bars of "Tantum Ergo," Father William planned his next day. He would go visit the elderly shut-ins at Over the Rainbow, a new nursing home that had just opened about three miles away and boasted, "A Special Neighborhood for the Memory Impaired."

* * * *

Francesca wanted to scream. It seemed Chip just couldn't stop talking and she was beginning to fear she would nod off in the middle of one of his endless soliloquies. She kept surreptitiously glancing at her watch, hoping that he would pause to take a breath and she could then remark on how late it was. But then she remembered the champagne in her refrigerator. *Is there any way to avoid inviting him in? Should I stage another headache?*

As the waitress stopped by to refill their water glasses, Chip continued droning on and on. So far, he had covered his early childhood in Mexico Beach, Florida, the various elementary schools he had attended, including the names of his most memorable teachers, descriptions of his childhood friends, and even the plot summaries of books that, he claimed, had "really shaped my character." They had been in Benedetti's nearly two hours, and he still hadn't even begun on high school!

The food, at least, was delicious. Francesca had wolfed down every bite of eggplant parmesan and had left not even a strand of linguine on the dish. She had devoured not one but two of the hot rolls, each one liberally slathered in butter. She'd also ordered the richest dessert she could find, reasoning that she might as well give herself some pleasure in the midst of this apparently endless agony. *I wonder if this is what Hell would be like: an eternity spent listening to some boring person drone on and on. But without the solace of food.*

As soon as the waitress placed the dessert on the table, Francesca took a generous bite of the succulent mocha layer cake that was billed as "sinfully delicious." *As long as it's not a mortal sin, I'm safe.*

A few moments later, almost as if someone had flipped a switch, Chip stopped talking about himself. "Look at the time! And we still have that champagne at your house."

She knew that now was the moment. Now was the time to tell him she would love to invite him in, but she just couldn't. She had to think of something, and fast. But he caught her off guard with his next remark.

"I really am looking forward to showing you some of the more detailed plans I have for the parish. I figured we could do that at your house, since we'd have more room to spread out the blueprints."

The word "blueprints" sounded a warning bell in her head. *What in the world would he be doing that would involve a blueprint? Is he planning to redesign the church?* There was no way she could put him off now.

* * * *

Maria let herself into the rectory kitchen, taking care not to make too much noise. It was getting late and she figured the priests upstairs might be sleeping. She didn't want to alarm them or make them think there was a burglar. She and her husband, Paul, had been to the movies, and he had agreed to wait in the car while she stopped in to check the freezer. The archbishop was coming for lunch the next day and everything had to be perfect. She wanted to make pork roast and thought there was one in the freezer, but she wanted to be sure. She tiptoed over to the freezer, pulled open the door, and began rummaging around. There were sirloin steaks, packages of chicken breasts, lamb chops, but no pork roast.

She opened her purse and looked around until she located her shopping list. She added "pork roast" and also realized she needed more flour and sugar as well. Just then, she froze. She heard a definite sound of something scratching in the corner of the kitchen. Her stomach clenched. Then she felt something furry with sharp little feet run across her foot. She let out a blood-curdling scream, dropped her purse, climbed up on the nearest chair, and stood there, cringing and shaking. She would stay there all night, she decided, rather than risk being attacked again by that mouse.

* * * *

Upstairs, Father Bunt was in his pajamas, saying his night prayers, when he heard the unmistakable sound of a woman screaming. He knew that only he and Father William were supposed to be in the rectory at this hour. Everyone else had gone home. Throwing on his robe, he headed down the stairs barefoot. He saw the light on in the kitchen and rushed through the door, praying he would not be walking in on a crime scene. There on the chair he saw Maria, white faced and weeping.

"Maria, what is it?"

But before she could answer, he let out a loud yell, because something had sunk its sharp teeth into his big toe.

* * * *

Father William sat bolt upright in bed. He was so used to the trains by now that he hardly flinched when one rumbled by, but the sound of a woman screaming had awakened him. He ran downstairs, only to be stunned by the sight of Maria standing on a chair with Father Bunt limping around the kitchen.

"William, I think a rat bit me. Don't they carry rabies?"

"Don't worry, Father, I'm sure it wasn't a rat. It had to be Ignatius, and hamsters never get rabies."

Father Bunt sat down and inspected his toe. "Well, that's a relief."

But Maria was a different story. "Father, I don't care if it's a rat or a hamster, I'm not getting down until someone catches it."

Just then, Father William spotted a familiar whiskery face peering out from beneath the cabinets. He fished in his bathrobe pocket and extracted a shelled pecan. Bending down, he held out his hand with the treat in full view, and the little animal came rushing over. But just as Ignatius was about to grab the pecan, things went all wrong. Dopey came running in, and Ignatius went zooming away. Father William watched in dismay as the dog knocked over the pail with hamster treats inside and proceeded to devour them. Then he stood there, tongue hanging out, looking pleased with himself.

The rectory doorbell rang, and Father Bunt went to answer it. Seconds later, in came Maria's husband with an expression on his face that indicated he was none too pleased to see his wife standing on a chair and two priests nearby in their bathrobes.

"What the hell is going on?" he demanded.

"Take it easy now," Father Bunt said. "It seems Maria got frightened by a hamster that's apparently on the loose in the rectory."

Paul walked over to the chair and helped Maria down. "Come on, Maria, let's go home. You're safe now."

After they had left and Father Bunt was back upstairs, Father William made sure Dopey was locked out of the kitchen overnight. Then he refilled the pail with goodies. *Now it's just a matter of waiting—and praying.*

* * * *

Francesca had downed a cup of strong coffee at the restaurant, so she no longer felt that she might fall asleep as Chip talked. They were at her house where he was making an elaborate show of opening the champagne bottle. He poured them each a glass of the bubbling golden liquid and then toasted her: "To the most beautiful woman at Saint Rita's Church!" Despite her annoyance with him, she found herself smiling. *I'm a sucker for compliments.*

Then he picked up a book from the coffee table, her collection of the letters of Flannery O'Connor. "*The Habit of Being*—what's up with that?"

She tried to give him a quick rundown of the life of one of her favorite authors, a Catholic woman who had lived in Milledgeville, Georgia, but as she spoke, she could see the interest dying in his eyes. Then a little spark went off in her brain and she decided to goad him.

"One of my favorite quotes from her is 'There's no such thing as a modern Catholic.'"

"Oh? When did she die?"

"1964."

He chuckled. "Well, that explains it. I'm sure if she were alive today, she'd have a different opinion."

Francesca stood up and returned the book to her shelves, mentally rolling her eyes. *He's impossible*. She turned around to see him unrolling what he called the blueprints but were actually his own penciled sketches.

"I've already shared these with a number of parishioners—a few folks on the parish council, some guys in the Knights of Columbus and, of course Father Bunt and Father William—and some of the old codger . . . er . . . seniors in the Golden Glories club."

"What did they think?"

He stopped to brush an invisible speck from his tie. "Oh, mostly quite positive. Yes, indeed, quite favorable."

She leaned in closer to see what the sketches were all about. There was Saint Rita's altar, but it looked very different. Then she realized why: he had penciled in a new area, very near the altar, for the choir to sit in. She saw Chip also had deleted the big crucifix centered over the altar.

"I don't understand. What happened to the crucifix?"

"Oh, that type is really old hat. We want to show the joy of the Resurrection, not the sadness of . . . well, you know . . . what came before."

He now extracted another sheet of paper with an image he had printed off the computer. "Now *this* is the kind of crucifix we need at Saint Rita's."

She blinked her eyes rapidly. The photo showed the figure of Jesus, but no cross. His muscular arms were outstretched in a gesture of triumph, and she couldn't help but think that He looked like someone about to leap off a diving board.

"It's the Resurrected Jesus," Chip explained proudly. "Joyful and contemporary. And this will really make a splash in the sanctuary."

She winced at his choice of words. She wondered if he had used the same description when he had presented his ideas to the others. Somehow she could not envision the Knights of Columbus members liking the idea of a new and "joyful" cross.

"So, what do you think?" He polished off the first glass of champagne, reached for the bottle, topped off her glass, and then refilled his own.

"I have to be honest with you, Chip. I'm much more traditional. I really like the crucifix we have now. Maybe it's not joyful, but it shows what really happened; you know . . ."

Chip didn't seem to be listening. Instead, he moved closer to her, causing a warning bell to sound in her mind.

"The Crucifixion?" As she uttered the word, Francesca pulled her hands in tightly toward her body, so he couldn't do a repeat performance of his surprise attack on her palm.

"You seem really uptight," he said. "What's going on with you?"

"Oh, nothing, really, I'm fine." She noticed her voice sounded squeaky and nervous, and probably unconvincing.

"Look, Francesca, there's no reason to be afraid of me. I don't bite, you know." Now he reached over and gently pushed a stray lock of hair off her forehead.

"Is it real serious with you and Tony?"

"We've been dating for a while, but, well, I mean, we're not engaged or anything."

He inched just a little bit closer. "Don't get me wrong; I don't want to pry, but you were married once, weren't you? I noticed the photos."

"Yes, I was—but he died."

Much to her dismay, the words brought tears to her eyes.

"Hey, no need to cry!" Chip put his arm around her shoulder.

There was something about his solidity, the musky scent of his cologne, that suddenly enticed her. She longed to be comforted, and he seemed to know it.

"Don't cry, darlin'," he whispered.

Then he pulled her into his arms and kissed her right on the lips. At first, she didn't resist, but then an image of Dean's face suddenly flashed in her mind. *This is all wrong.*

She drew back, and then stood up. "Chip, really, I think it's time you left."

He stood up too. "Look, I'm sorry if I came on too strong . . ."

"It's just that it's late and I'm tired."

"Sure, I can take the hint."

And much to her relief, he gathered up his papers and left.

* * * *

Father Bunt rose before dawn the next day. He wanted to be sure everything was in order for Archbishop Reginald MacPherson's arrival at the rectory. He looked down at his bandaged toe and suddenly remembered the night before. *Oh, Lord, I hope Maria will show up. We really need her today.*

He quickly went over in his mind the list of guests he had invited to the luncheon. There was Father William, of course, plus Mrs. Reedley from the Golden Glories club; a man from the Knights of Columbus whose name he couldn't remember; Margaret Hennessy, newly retired; Robert Adams, the president of the parish council; and Sister Therese, the principal of Saint Rita's school. Maria had told him she would be making appetizers, pork roast, biscuits, fried okra, and other vegetables that he couldn't remember, and her famous blueberry pie for dessert. *But what if she doesn't show up?*

That possibility was just too terrible to contemplate, so he put it out of his mind. He made a mental note of the things he wanted to discuss with the archbishop in private. After lunch they would have coffee in Father Bunt's study and probably spend a half hour together. He wanted to let the archbishop know that he was doing a good job at Saint Rita's but without bragging or seeming pompous. He went into his office and quickly logged into the church accounts, writing down a few figures. He could certainly assure the archbishop that collections were steady, although he suspected his boss would have been more delighted to hear that they were rising. He would not mention the controversy over the new liturgist. *Surely things will calm down soon.*

He wondered why Archbishop MacPherson had set up this meeting. Was it just a social visit? The archbishop had grown up in the same small town in northern Michigan as

Father Bunt's dad, and the two men still talked on the phone now and again. When MacPherson had been named archbishop of Atlanta, five years before, Father Bunt's dad had called his old friend and said, "Take good care of my boy." The archbishop had come for informal visits at Father Bunt's other parishes now and again and always treated him with kindness. But Father Bunt still retained a healthy respect for a man who held a great deal of power in the archdiocese, especially when it came to priests' assignments.

But had MacPherson gotten wind of problems at the parish? Had a parishioner perhaps written a letter of complaint to the chancery? It was something that Father Bunt had dreaded during all his years as a pastor. So far, he had managed to head off complaints before people got so riled that they decided to go over his head. Was his luck changing now?

He looked at his to-do list for the day and saw "Call Chip" at the top. He had already left three phone messages with the man, and none had been returned. *Well, maybe he's out of town.*

That was the charitable response to this kind of oversight: give the person the benefit of the doubt. He was sure he would hear from Chip very soon. Dressing quickly, he picked up his breviary and read the prayers for the morning. Then he heard some encouraging sounds from downstairs. It was Maria greeting that ridiculous beast she had adopted: "Dopey, how's my big, sweet boy today?"

I hope he's housebroken by now, Father Bunt thought sourly as he headed downstairs for breakfast.

* * * *

Father William crossed himself after leaving the kitchen. He had just told Maria a big, fat lie, but what else could he have done? He knew the archbishop was coming for lunch, and he knew she wouldn't be comfortable in the kitchen if she thought the "big rat" was still on the loose, so he had assured her that Ignatius was safely back in his cage upstairs. *How I wish that were true*. She had looked so relieved that it had made him feel even guiltier. But he knew Father Bunt was apprehensive about the archbishop's visit, and Father William didn't want Maria's fears of a renegade hamster to spoil everything. Besides, Ignatius usually slept most of the day.

Father William decided to stop by the adoration chapel for a few moments of silence before lunch, but as he opened the door, he was startled by the sound of guitar music. *Another blasted innovation, no doubt compliments of Chip*. He tried to concentrate on his prayers as best he could, then crossed himself, genuflected, and left. Outside, he was approached by two young mothers who had children in the school. The first one, whose name he couldn't recall, was clearly upset.

"Father, why don't we have the *Confiteor* during Mass anymore?"

Father William took a deep breath. He missed the long penitential rite himself, but Chip had said it took too much time.

"I wish we could have it, I really do, but it's out of my hands."

"But Father, you're the assistant pastor, aren't you?"

It was then that he explained the new chain of command. When he did, the second woman, Amelia Brown, didn't mince words. "Well, I think that's wrong, Father! Why should this . . . this Chip person have control over what you do?"

He shrugged his shoulders. It was clear further discussion would lead nowhere.

"It's just the way it is. I wish I could do something, but . . ."

He hurried off to the nursing home, feeling helpless.

* * * *

The archbishop rang the doorbell precisely at 11:30. Father Bunt was there in seconds to let him in. Archbishop MacPherson was 70, and it was rumored that he would soon be retiring. He was a short, stocky man with pure white hair trimmed in a jaunty crew cut. He had a few deep lines on his face, but Father Bunt judged him strong and fit. As Father Bunt showed the archbishop a few changes that had been made in the rectory since Father John had left, he made a mental note to start exercising himself, as he had looked in the mirror only that morning and noticed the beginnings of a pot belly. *As soon as things settle down here a bit, I'll start jogging or take up tennis or something.*

When they went into the downstairs sitting room, Father Bunt was horrified to see Dopey lounging about on the Queen Anne recliner, enthusiastically scratching fleas. He started to call for Maria to take the dog outside, but MacPherson stopped him. The archbishop leaned down and began petting the mangy beast and talking to him in an affectionate tone.

"I had a dog like this when I was a boy. Your father might remember him. He was mostly poodle but had a bit of Labrador and German shepherd as well. We called him Rex. What's this fine fellow's name?"

Father Bunt stared at a small hole in the carpet. "It's, ah, Dopey."

The archbishop's brow furrowed. "Well, who named him *that*?

"Uh, the children did, over at the school."

Now the lines on the older man's face smoothed over. "Well, as long as the children like it, it will have to do!" He smiled. "Dopey indeed!"

At the stroke of noon, Father Bunt ushered the archbishop into the dining room, where the others were gathering. He made the introductions, and everyone stood while the archbishop asked God's blessing on the food. Then Maria swept in carrying the appetizers: small pastries filled with bits of seasoned beef and vegetables. Father Bunt knew that everything was "from scratch" because Maria had made a point of telling him, more than once, that she served nothing that came from mixes. The archbishop evidently remembered Maria from a previous visit and lavished praise on her culinary skills.

Then, as Maria was serving the salads, into the room rushed Chip. "I'm really sorry I'm so late, Your Grace," he said, reaching out to shake hands with the archbishop. "I was in my office ordering DVDs for the new engaged couples program, and the time just got away from me."

Father Bunt glanced nervously at the other diners. Mrs. Reedley looked like she had just swallowed a raw turnip, while the fellow from the Knights of Columbus whose name he'd forgotten again was clenching his lips in what looked like an attempt to keep silent. Father Bunt knew they weren't the only diners who had lodged complaints against Chip.

Maria quickly put down another place setting, and Chip put his napkin in his lap with a flourish. Taking a sip of iced tea, he addressed Sister Therese, who was sitting across from him.

"I don't think we've met. I'm Chip Cambio, the new liturgist."

"I'm Sister Therese. Pleased to meet you." She gave him the ghost of a smile.

Father Bunt was just about to comment on the fine flavor of the salad dressing when to his horror he heard Chip say to Sister, "Well, I see you are still wearing the old habit, bless your heart. I'm always interested in hearing from sisters who haven't chosen the more . . . uh . . . modern form of dress."

All eyes turned to Sister Therese now, including the archbishop's. Father Bunt could feel his blood pressure rising. Sister Therese did not suffer fools gladly. Would she hold her tongue with the archbishop present?

Now he noticed a strange glint in Sister's eyes. "Well, Mr. Cambio, let's put it this way: I just look terrible in polyester pant suits."

A few people coughed, and Mrs. Reedley took a sip of water and began choking. This was enough to steer Chip away from the conversation. He stood up and began pounding Mrs. Reedley on the back until she shooed him away with some elaborate arm gestures.

"So you're the new liturgist here, is that right?" the archbishop asked, once everyone had resumed eating their salads. "What exactly are you in charge of?"

Father Bunt felt a grape tomato settle like a stone in his stomach.

"Well, sir, I'm in charge of musical selections, plus programs for engaged and married couples, and I also give Baptism classes, and, let's see . . ." He studied his hand as if his list of duties were inscribed there.

"I oversee special liturgies for holy days. Oh yes, and of course I train lectors, Eucharistic ministers, and dancers."

"Dancers?" The archbishop took a sip of water.

Chip tore a roll in two and slathered it with butter. "Yes, sir. At my last parish, we had some beautiful rhythmic processions. As you know," he said in a familiar tone, as if he were finally getting a chance to talk shop with a peer, "Church teaching says we must practice enculturation in the liturgy."

The archbishop stared back at Chip but didn't say a word. At that moment, as if answering Father Bunt's silent prayers, the man from the Knights of Columbus changed the topic, telling the archbishop about a basketball tournament they would be sponsoring for the children of the parish.

The meal continued with pleasant small talk. But as the main course was winding down, Chip jumped back into the limelight, pulling out a big pad of paper, which he called his "blueprint for the future," and displaying it in the center of the table. Margaret Hennessy, who managed to keep her aplomb no matter what was going on around her, said pleasantly, "Oh, you've been very busy."

Father Bunt felt as if he were a character in a play who had forgotten his lines. Every time he tried to steer the conversation, Chip grabbed the reins instead.

"Some of you have already seen the plans." Chip's eyes swept over the table. "But for those who haven't, I can mention that Saint Rita's will have a new, more joyful crucifix, plus we'll remove the statues and the kneelers—and, oh yes, make more room for the choir up front."

The archbishop put down his fork and raised his eyebrows at Father Bunt. As Chip continued talking about his plans to "breathe the Spirit into the parish," Father Bunt felt his anger rising, but he wanted to remain calm in front of the archbishop. Chip was going too far this time. He had never once mentioned plans to remove the statues and the kneelers, not to mention changing the crucifix.

"What's wrong with statues and kneelers?" Mrs. Reedley inquired in an icy tone. Chip opened his mouth, took a deep breath, and launched into an explanation.

Father Bunt glanced wearily at his watch. Lunch couldn't end soon enough.

* * * *

Father William was sitting quietly, pushing a chunk of fried okra around his plate while praying that the conflict would soon be over. He hated to see this kind of thing happen, especially in the archbishop's presence. But as he raised his fork to his mouth, his attention suddenly was diverted as he spotted a familiar whiskered face in the corner of the dining room. *Ignatius!*

While the others were getting up to eye Chip's plans, Father William quietly went over and scooped up the little fellow. He was just about to sneak out of the room without anyone noticing him, when Chip suddenly looked at him and yelled, "Father, is that a mouse?"

The next few moments were chaos. A blueberry pie went sailing across the table, as Maria, who had just entered the room to serve dessert, squealed and then fell to the floor in a dead faint. Father William reached out to catch her—too late—and Ignatius took advantage of his distraction, springing from his hand and landing on the thick carpet. As he knelt to tend to Maria, Father William glimpsed the little creature scurrying through the open door and into the kitchen. *Oh, Lord! He's on the loose again.*

* * * *

Later that day, as he prepared to celebrate the 5:30 p.m. Mass, Father Bunt thanked God that the archbishop had a sense of humor. He also thanked God that Maria had made three pies, so dessert eventually had been served anyway. The archbishop evidently had seen train wrecks like the luncheon before, and Father Bunt thought it had to be obvious that Chip had been an uninvited guest. He had hoped to talk with the archbishop right after lunch, but another appointment had called the man away immediately. *Maybe that was for the best.* Now Father Bunt was concerned that Archbishop MacPherson would think Chip had too much power in the parish. Then his conscience spoke up: *And who gave him the power?*

Father Bunt leaned his head against his hands and thought about the words that he said every day at Mass: "Lord, cleanse me from my iniquities; wash me of my sins." He had made a big mistake. Chip had only been at the parish a short while and had already managed to wreak havoc. Six months could prove completely deadly.

* * * *

Francesca looked through the stack of library books by her chair and realized two were overdue. She had planned a long, lazy Sunday afternoon at home, but now she picked up her car keys, intending to drive over to the Decatur library, before putting them down again. *I should walk; I can burn off some calories*. She dug through her purse to make sure she had her cell phone and library card—and immediately started to panic. Her wallet was gone. She did a frantic search of the house before concluding it had to be in the bottom drawer of her desk at the rectory. She'd found it there before, fallen out of her usually overstuffed purse.

She started walking in the direction of the library, taking a short detour over to Saint Rita's to look for the wallet. Noticing there were no cars parked outside the rectory, she figured no one was there and let herself in with her master key. She rushed over to her desk and opened the bottom drawer, breathing a huge sigh of relief when she spied her wallet. She locked the door behind her as she left.

As she stepped outside, she looked across the empty school playground and caught a glimpse of a man in the distance talking with a woman in a habit. They were too far away for her to hear what they were saying, but they seemed to be gesturing angrily at each other. Curiosity got the best of her, and she edged her way slowly across the playground, trying to avoid being seen. As she drew closer, she saw that the man was Chip, but the nun's back was turned so she couldn't see her face. They were so engrossed in their discussion they didn't seem to notice her as she hid behind one of the gigantic oaks on the perimeter of the playground.

"Oh, you're totally wrong and you know it," the nun said.

Chip jabbed his finger toward her as if bringing home a point. "Your problem, Sister, is you're just too set in your ways!"

At that moment, Chip seemed to glance in the direction of the tree, and Francesca got nervous about being seen. She edged her way carefully toward the sidewalk, dodging behind trees so she wouldn't be detected. *I don't want them to think I'm snooping on them.* And then she blushed as she realized that, of course, that was exactly what she was doing. As she got onto the sidewalk, she saw them still together in the distance, continuing their argument. Now the nun was shaking her fist.

* * * *

That evening, Francesca opened her front door, and there was Tony standing on the porch, looking apologetic. They both started talking at once, and then laughed.

"Come on in," she said. "You talk first."

He sat down in the rocking chair. "Well, I just want to apologize for overreacting when I saw you and . . . whatshisname . . . *Chip* . . . the other night. After all, we're not . . . well, married, and you certainly have the right to see other men."

Somehow this wasn't what she had hoped to hear. She really didn't want Tony giving her free rein to date other men because that would mean he might date other women, and she didn't want that.

She settled down on the couch next to Tubs. "Tony, I'm not dating Chip. He barged into a Choir Chicks' meeting, and we had supper one time. I was curious to see what his plans are for the parish, that's all."

Tony looked relieved. "Well, as far as I'm concerned, we can just put it all behind us." Then he hesitated. "What are his plans, exactly?"

She stood up. "Let me get you a drink. This might take a while."

CHAPTER 7

Sister Therese was in the school library with four of the other Dominican sisters when Chip showed up unexpectedly with a dog on a leash.

"Sorry to barge in on you like this, ladies," Chip said.

"Oh, that's perfectly fine." Sister Therese wished he would refer to them by the title they preferred, which was, of course, "sisters," but she smiled at him and hoped she looked sincere. She reminded herself of a saying she had once heard: for some people, you may be the only reflection of Christ they meet. But this man had a way of getting on her last nerve.

Chip bustled into the room carrying a large cardboard box. It was a muggy day, and his face was ruddy from exertion. There were the faintest beginnings of perspiration stains on his blue shirt.

He tugged at the leash. "Ladies, meet my dog, Wormwood. He's a little . . . feisty, so best not to pet him."

As if on cue, the dog bared his teeth at Sister Therese and let out a low growl. Chip put the box down on a table with a flourish and then tied the leash to one of the chairs. The dog collapsed on the floor, panting.

"Sister Therese, I know it's a bit early to be thinking about Christmas, but I figured the children would need plenty of time to rehearse."

Christmas was her favorite time of year, and Sister Therese relished getting a head start on it.

"Well, Chip, it's really never too early to think about Christmas . . ."

"I thought you would see it that way. Now, let me tell you my plans . . . that is, if you ladies have time?"

Sister Therese thought about all the tasks awaiting her in the next few hours, all the lessons she needed to prepare for tomorrow, all the prayers, Mass, supper, Benediction. She glanced at the other sisters, who seemed to be thinking along the same lines.

"Of course we have time."

The sisters squeezed into the child-sized library chairs. "Well, I have a really exciting Christmas program planned this year. If you ladies will take a look at these booklets . . ." He handed them out, while the dog began snoring loudly.

Sister Therese took a deep breath. She had always been the one to oversee the Christmas program in the parish, and the other sisters had delighted in coaching little children to represent angels, the Wise Men, Saint Joseph, and the Virgin Mary. *But maybe Father Bunt wants the liturgist to take over this year. After all, it seems he's taken over everything else.*

"If you ladies will take a look at the first page, you'll see the list of characters we'll need for the pageant. Of course, there will be the baby, the mother, the father . . . uh, that is,

Joseph . . . and the animals, but we're moving into something new and different this year."

Sister Therese could feel her heart rate quickening in anger. *What could be new and different about the Incarnation? God, help me to control myself.*

But as she glanced at the list of "characters," she feared her temper was about to reach the boiling point. To the usual nativity cast had been added Santa Claus, Frosty the Snowman, Rudolph the Red-Nosed Reindeer, and the Care Bears.

"Chip, why do you have Care Bears and Frosty and . . . and . . . all these others in the manger?"

He laughed in a way that made her momentarily feel like slapping him. "I've heard that question many times before, but let me assure you, the children just love this approach to Christmas. You see, this is a way to emphasize inclusiveness." He pronounced the word as if it were sacred.

"Inclusiveness?" Sister Therese choked out the word. She could see the other sisters staring down at the table, perhaps because they were afraid to catch her eye.

"Yes, and equality, too. You see, I envision little boys having a chance to play the role of Mary, and little girls playing Joseph." He rolled up his sleeves. "This way, they get the important message."

Sister put her hand on the crucifix affixed to the rosary beads on her waist and squeezed till her knuckles turned white.

"The message?"

"Yes, you know, the whole message of Christmas! It's a time when people of all nationalities, ages, religions, gender preferences, and races come together in a spirit of peace and fun."

Sister Therese knew sarcasm was one of her sins, but she couldn't stop the words that flew out of her mouth.

"And all these years I thought the message of Christmas had to do with God becoming man. I wasn't aware that *gender preferences* had anything to do with it."

She heard a definite giggle, combined with a fake cough, emanating from Sister Josephine, the youngest nun seated at the table. Chip, however, ignored the reaction.

"Look, Sister, we both know Christmas is for kids. They love Rudolph, Santa, and the Care Bears. We need to make it more relevant for them."

Sister could feel the faint beginnings of a headache pinging at her temple. "Chip, for Heaven's sakes, I've never had a child complain that Christmas wasn't . . . wasn't . . . relevant. They don't need Care Bears and"—she glanced at the list again—"SpongeBob, for God's sake!"

She didn't think she could be more annoyed by him, but the smirk on his face changed her mind. He didn't say a word, just stood there, staring as if he pitied her. She counted to five before speaking again.

"And what would the sisters' role be in this . . . in this . . . performance?"

He began rummaging in the box. "I have a great plan for you, ladies! I really want to jazz up the Christmas music this year. No more of those old tired religious carols."

Hail Mary, full of grace, the Lord is with thee. Sister Therese began saying the Rosary silently in an effort to control her temper.

Chip pulled a cluster of tambourines from the box. "Ladies, these instruments will really put some punch into the pageant.

And you have plenty of time to learn how to play them." He perched on one of the library tables with a triumphant, what-do-you-think-of-*this* grin on his face.

As Sister Therese was about to speak, the dog chose that precise moment to very loudly pass gas. There was more coughing from the sisters at the table, as Chip stood up.

"Oh, I almost forgot! As long as I have all you ladies here together, there's something else we need to discuss. It's about your . . . ," he said as he tilted his head sadly, ". . . well, your outfits."

"Outfits?" She was only capable of repeating what he had said, in the hope that she had heard him wrong.

"Look, I can't tell you what to wear. That's not my jurisdiction. But I'd love for Saint Rita's to look more contemporary—and you ladies could take the lead. After all, the kids look up to you. I'm sure they wonder why you're dressed in those floor-length gowns and those black head thingies."

Sister Therese slammed her hand down on the table. Her heart was shuddering dangerously in her chest. She knew her face was bright red and she knew she was losing it.

"Those GOWNS, MR. CAMBIO, and . . . and . . . HEAD THINGIES are called religious habits!"

At the sound of her voice, the dog awakened and let out a low growl, but Chip seemed unfazed.

"Oh, sure, I know that, but they just look old-fashioned." He smiled at her as if she were a dotty old woman who still called cars "horseless carriages." There was no stopping him.

Chip's idiotic smile drove her over the edge. She stood up and rushed toward him. At first she made as if to slap him, but at the last minute she merely grabbed his arm and started to drag him out of the room. The dog started growling and baring its teeth at her.

"Really, Sister, you don't have to get pushy," Chip said angrily. He extricated himself roughly from her grip.

"Come on, Wormwood, let's get out of here."

* * * *

Francesca hated to eavesdrop, but she couldn't help it. Her desk was positioned just a few feet away from the tiny reception room, where the priests usually met with people planning weddings, Baptisms, and funerals. The door was open today, and she could hear every word. But the person talking with the young couple about their upcoming wedding wasn't a priest; it was Chip. She thought it odd that he would be in charge of weddings, but maybe that was one of the typical duties of a liturgist.

She had seen the young couple come in a few moments earlier. She judged them to be in their early twenties. Right after they had seated themselves, she had seen Chip come rushing in, and had heard him introducing himself. Now she could catch snippets of the conversation.

"We'd like Mindy's father to give her away, of course," she heard the future groom say.

There was a silence and the sound of rustling papers, and then Chip's voice. "Well, that's how it was done in the old days, of course, but if you take a look at this booklet, you'll see how weddings are being updated here at Saint Rita's."

After a few seconds, she heard the woman's voice: "So the bride's father doesn't accompany her to the altar?"

"No, as you'll see from this document, we'd like the entire wedding party to process up the aisle together. This means the bride, the groom, the various groomsmen, bridesmaids, plus the parents. It's more equal that way."

The future bride's voice sounded squeaky now. "But can't we have it the more traditional way if we want?"

There was a huge sigh, which Francesca figured was coming from Chip. He spoke next.

"Tradition is fine, of course, when it comes to older people, but you're both young. And for your wedding you want . . . something vibrant . . . creative . . . your own way of doing things!"

There was more silence and the sound of rustling pages. Then Francesca heard the man clearing his throat. "About these vows: We were thinking more along the line of the standard vows."

And then Chip's voice: "You mean until death do us part and all that?"

"Yes, that would be it."

She couldn't see Chip's face, but she could imagine the expression. He had a way of raising an eyebrow to indicate utter astonishment at what he was hearing.

"Take a look at these modern vows," she heard Chip say, and then heard him reading aloud:

"Do you, so-and-so, in the respect and confidence of your own individuality, acknowledge within yourself that same respect and confidence for this woman, so-and-so, in the certainty that you will share the deepest of all your emotions: aware also that you may share, but not know, for in knowing you deny the person that she is?"

The man's voice was now somewhat louder than before: "But what does that mean . . . denying the person that she is? And what about sickness and health, and death do us part?"

"What I'm getting at here is you want to write your *own* vows," Chip said. "This is just an example. Why use something that's been used before? The vows should be an expression of your unique relationship."

A long silence followed. Francesca imagined the couple whispering to each other.

Then the man's voice: "Well, is this what other couples are doing now?"

She heard Chip's reassuring voice: "Parishes have been using vows like these for *many* years."

There was another silence, and then she heard Chip: "So you take this booklet home and talk it over, and we'll have another meeting."

And then the woman's voice, rather shrill: "This booklet says at the bottom that the ceremony is taken from a Unitarian Web site! Aren't we having a Catholic wedding?"

The phone rang then, so she couldn't hear Chip's reply, but he must have assuaged the woman's fears, because when the couple emerged from the room 15 minutes later, they were smiling. Chip was his usual confident and cheerful self.

"Well, thank you, Chip," the man said. "I have to admit we hadn't thought about adapting the old vows. Like you said, this is *our* wedding, and we want to be as original as possible. We'll spend some time thinking about your suggestions."

Oh, no, they've drunk Chip's Kool-Aid.

* * * *

As the weeks wore on, Francesca judged the situation at Saint Rita's to be growing progressively more dismal. She found herself approaching Sundays with misgivings in her heart. What would Chip try next? She had considered attending Mass elsewhere, but something in her resisted. This was, after all, the church where Dean had been received into the Faith, and it was the place where she felt at home in the community.

Today she settled uneasily in the pew next to Tony. *I'll be darned if I'm going to leave here just because of Chip*, she thought. And then, as the stream of angry thoughts began, she crossed herself and knelt down. *Lord, I know where anger comes from, and it isn't from you. Please help me to keep things in perspective. I know there are people all over the world who can't get to Mass because of persecution and violence. There are people whose homes have been destroyed by earthquakes and fires. This is a small annoyance by comparison.*

But then, all her resolve, all her prayerful thoughts dissolved when the lector, a thin woman in her forties, walked up to the pulpit and began to emote, her voice rising and falling precipitously as she read each line from the lectionary. Seemingly unaware of the scriptural message she was delivering, the woman focused on adding elaborate flourishes to random syllables. Francesca cringed at the shrill, almost unintelligible rendering of Saint Paul's gentle words.

As they were leaving the church that day, Francesca saw Chip talking with the woman.

"Good work! That really put some pizzazz in it! Your delivery was the perfect touch!"

The woman was beaming.

"Pizzazz," Tony echoed dismally as they headed out the door. "I guess he's also in charge of the lectors, right?" He picked up a bulletin and looked at her quizzically. "Shouldn't we go to another parish?"

"No, then that would mean Chip wins. This is my church—and yours now, too. We're going to stick it out. My feeling is that his days are numbered here."

"What do you mean?"

"We're not the only people who are angry. I can sense it all around us. I bet it won't be long before he heads to another parish and we'll have our beautiful Mass back again."

They walked to Tony's truck parked down the street. "I hope you're right, Francesca. I gotta be honest with you. I was away from the Catholic Church an awfully long time, and this kind of stuff isn't exactly helping my . . ." Here he searched for a word.

"I know what you mean, Tony. The piano music, the . . . pizzazz, the insipid songs . . . they just make it more difficult to pray and focus on what's happening on the altar."

Tony helped her into the truck and sat for a moment, drumming his fingers on the steering wheel.

"Yeah, it's definitely more difficult. It's like . . . well, what is it the Church teaches about how we all carry crosses, we all suffer, like Christ did?"

She put on her seatbelt and nodded at him. "Yes, Chip is definitely a cross."

* * * *

The next day, Francesca was answering phones in the rectory while also enjoying a few flashbacks. The night before, she and Tony had gone for a late supper at Benedetti's, where he had treated her to a delicious meal. Afterward, they had driven to the Bruster's ice cream shop for dessert. The evening had ended very late on a romantic note with him kissing her and calling her "sweetheart."

The pleasant memories dissolved as Father Bunt came down the stairs, looking disheveled and disturbed. His hair was sticking out in various directions and he had not shaved. He took a seat near her desk and seemed to be trying to compose himself.

"Father, is something wrong?"

He pulled out a small, dark book from his pocket, which looked like a prayer book, and held it tightly in his hands. "Something is terribly wrong, my dear. I hate to be the bearer of such terrible news, but it seems that . . . it seems that Chip Cambio is dead."

"Dead!" She felt a clenching feeling in her stomach. Ever since her husband's car accident two years before, the mention of sudden death brought on a strong reaction.

"Oh, Father, I'm so sorry. What happened?"

He put down the little book, took out a big white handkerchief from his other pocket, and blew his nose. At that moment, Francesca saw Maria come out of the kitchen wearing a sunny expression and carrying a tray of steaming biscuits. But then she must have noticed their faces because she put the tray down and didn't say a word.

Father Bunt remained woodenly in the chair. Francesca had never seen him look so weary.

"Maria, I was just telling Francesca that we've had some very bad news. It seems that, well, I hate to say it, but Chip is dead."

Francesca noticed that the blood drained quickly from Maria's face, and she put her hand over her mouth but said nothing.

"He was found in the school library late last night by the custodian. It seems that a very heavy book case fell on him, somehow, and must have, well, must have hit him very hard on the head." Father Bunt paused. "Actually, we won't know all the details until the coroner's office gives us a report."

Now he pulled out his rosary beads from his pocket and intertwined them in his hands. "From what I have heard so far, the police suspect foul play."

Maria gasped. "You mean that someone . . . that someone . . ." Her voice trailed off.

"Yes, it looks like this horrible thing was intentional. Someone killed our liturgist."

CHAPTER 8

Francesca sat quietly at her desk, trying to compose herself. Father Bunt was back in his office, and Maria had returned to the kitchen. The phones were ringing off the hook: word of Chip's death had evidently gotten out through the parish grapevine. Francesca felt terrible about what had happened. True, Chip had been a royal pain, a big bore, and a definite thorn in the side of many parishioners. But he had been a handsome man who had brought her flowers and cat treats for Tubs. At that memory, she felt tears welling up in her eyes. She thought of all the things she didn't know about Chip. Despite his droning on and on about his life, she couldn't remember if he had ever mentioned his parents. Were they alive or dead? Did he have brothers and sisters? Had he ever been married?

She hated wading into a sea of regrets. She thought of her Aunt Rose, who had fought bitterly with her husband for many years. After he died, though, Aunt Rose was stricken with amnesia about his faults, describing him as if he were on the fast track to Sainthood. When Francesca's mother finally challenged Rose—"For Heaven's sake, woman, all you two ever did was fight!"—Rose just got angry. *I hope I'm not following in Aunt Rose's footsteps.*

Still, how could she help but feel somewhat guilty about all her angry thoughts about Chip? Of course, she wasn't the only one who'd been angry: Father Bunt said the police suspected foul play. Could someone in the parish have been angry enough to *kill* him? She shuddered at the thought and then jumped as the shrill bleating of the phone stemmed her tide of thoughts. This time it was Tony. Of course, he would have known about the death, since he investigated homicide cases, which were generally few and far between in Decatur.

"Francesca, how are you doing?" His tone was gentle. She knew he was trying to figure out if she already had heard the awful news.

"I've been better, Tony, I have to admit. I suppose you know about Chip?"

"Yeah, that's why I was calling. It's a terrible thing, really. I mean, he wasn't my favorite guy, obviously, but he sure didn't deserve what happened to him."

Francesca nervously twirled the phone cord around her hand. "What exactly did happen? All I heard was something about a book case."

"Well, I'd rather not talk about it over the phone. Why don't we have lunch tomorrow, and I'll fill you in on some details that will probably be hitting the newspapers soon anyway?"

Francesca's shift ended the next day at noon, and she met Tony for lunch at the Lebanese Grill on North Decatur road, a tiny café a few doors down from Clouds, a health-food store that she and her husband had frequented in their vegetarian days. All that had changed when she fell prey to a series of illnesses. When her doctor had gently hinted that her immune system would improve if she would eat meat once in a while, she had jumped on that excuse to devour steaks and eschew tofu, which she had come to hate.

As they ate, Tony talked about the case, although he cautioned her against sharing the information with others, at least until it became public knowledge. It seems that Chip had moved all the hardbound red hymnals to the book shelves in the school library. He had told the librarian the books would be sent out shortly for rebinding, and then returned to the pews.

"According to Sister Therese, however, Chip's real plans were quite different." Tony sipped his iced tea. "He had confided to her one day that he wanted to get rid of the books entirely, to 'bring the parish into the 21st century,' but he didn't want to deal with fallout from parishioners, so I guess that's why he concocted the rebinding story."

"So do you think the idea was to leave the books in the library until people stopped asking about them and then get rid of them?"

Tony speared a piece of the feta cheese that adorned his Greek salad. "I think that was the plan—and he was in there on the night he died, packing up the books and implementing the plan."

"But why did he tell Sister? Surely he didn't think she would approve?"

Tony shrugged. "Beats me. He may not have realized just how strongly she felt about tradition. You've got to admit he was pretty obtuse about a lot of things."

Francesca buttered a slice of pita bread. "So you've talked with Sister?"

"Just briefly. She admitted she was extremely irritated with Chip at times, but she also seemed upset about his death." Tony paused for another sip of tea. "They had a few run-ins, though. He used to goad her about wearing the habit—and he was planning some big changes to the Christmas pageant, which was her turf."

Francesca remembered Sister's obvious anger outside the chapel. Her brow furrowed. "You don't think that Sister . . . that she had anything to do with his death?"

"I've learned over the years never to rule out anyone as a suspect. You'd be amazed at the people who can turn violent when they get angry enough." He handed her the plate of fried potatoes. "Although I have to admit Sister Therese is hard to picture as . . . well, you know, as a murderer."

Now he stopped eating and picked up the salt shaker, turning it over absently in his hand. "But she did admit that she had lost her temper with him more than once. And she evidently had told him she thought liturgists should be dressed as court jesters."

Francesca stopped in midbite. "What did he think about that remark, I wonder?"

"Well, according to Sister, the man did have a sense of humor."

Tony had ordered fried calamari for them to share. Even if she couldn't bear to think she was eating something as gruesome looking as a squid, she had to admit that the tender fried rings, crisp and golden, tasted delicious. As for the tentacles, she decided to leave those for Tony, who apparently relished them.

"So it actually was the . . . the *Worship II* hymnals that killed him?" Francesca asked.

Tony nodded. "You know those books weigh a ton." There was a moment of silence as Francesca contemplated the irony.

Tony drained his glass of iced tea and reached for another slice of the steamed pita bread. "Unfortunately, we have no real suspects yet, although it's still in the early days."

She prodded a calamari ring with her fork. "You're thinking someone must have pushed the shelves over, right?"

"That's what we're looking into. We're trying to determine who could have gotten into the school library at night. And here's something odd: Father Bunt said he didn't realize Chip himself had a master key to every office at the church. We found it in his pocket."

* * * *

Maria sat morosely in the kitchen with Dopey, snoring loudly just inches from her feet. She broke off a bit of biscuit and liberally frosted it with the softened butter that sat in the nearby dish. She tried to keep butter at room temperature because when it was cold, it had a tendency to rip the delicate crumbly flesh of the biscuits. Now she ate the biscuit almost automatically, forgoing her usual mental critique of her own cooking. Typically by this time of morning she would already be well into plans for lunch, but today seemed different. She hated to admit it, but she missed having the tall, good-looking Chip come sweeping in, sometimes carrying a bag of ripe berries—"in case you want to make a pie"—and other times handing her a cluster of fragrant flowers. She knew that she shouldn't have accepted gifts from the man, but he seemed harmless enough.

Her husband, Paul, didn't see it that way. He had not been at all pleased when he discovered the roses that Chip had given her, and he told her that he wanted "that damn Romeo" to stay away from her. Fortunately, she had never told Paul about the day Chip had started putting the moves on her in the kitchen because he would never understand, and it would only make matters worse.

She and Paul had been married ten years and had four children, but he still was a mystery to her. He had abruptly stopped going to church with her about five years before, and no amount of pleading on her part would change his mind. Lately, he had become especially moody, and he had said, more than once, that he didn't want her working in the rectory anymore, since he didn't trust priests. But they needed the money, so he didn't press her on quitting.

They had weathered their share of troubles over the years. Shortly after the birth of their first child, he'd started drinking more than usual, often spending his evenings at the local pub. Sometimes he'd get into fights—and one night he even landed in jail. *Thank God the charges were dropped.* As the years wore on, though, he'd gotten control of the drinking and become a doting and protective father to their children. But for some reason, he'd always had a jealous streak when it came to her, and it didn't seem that would ever change.

A train rumbled by, momentarily startling her. Then she felt a chilly, wet nose nudging at her ankle and looked down into the mournful eyes of Dopey. She buttered a chunk of biscuit and offered it to him. It vanished into the big, slobbering mouth in seconds. He then stood up, wagged his tail with great enthusiasm, and put his awkward fuzzy paws on the table to indicate that he wanted more.

There was no way she could be blue for long when Dopey was around. She fed him another snack, this time a bowl of leftover grits from breakfast, and then picked up her purse and began looking for a good recipe for tomorrow's supper. As she was searching, she found something in the recesses of the bag that made her gasp.

* * * *

Upstairs, Father Bunt sat at his desk, absently gazing at the framed photo that showed his parents on their wedding day. He remembered how joyful his mother had been when he told her about his decision to enter the seminary, but how disappointed his father had seemed. His father had wanted him to go into accounting or computers, "something practical," and had said more than once that he thought the priesthood was all wrong for him. His father was a no-nonsense sort of man, and he wanted his only son to carry on the Bunt family name.

One of his sisters had hyphenated her last name upon marriage in an effort to placate their father, but "Susan Bunt-Brown" didn't do the trick. To this day, whenever his parents visited, Father Bunt detected a note of sadness and disappointment in his father's eyes. Still, during all the years of his priesthood, Father Bunt had toiled endlessly to dot every I and cross every T, and perhaps some psychologist would claim he was trying to please his dad. *An impossible task.*

Now he stared grimly at the bushy-browed man in the wedding photo who, even in his twenties, had looked like someone you would not want to cross. Once this dreadful situation hit the newspapers, he would be sure to get a call from his mother, and his dad would be inches away from her on the other end of the line. The one thing that he would never say aloud, of course, would be, "I told you so. I told you that if you became a priest, it would be a disaster. Why didn't you listen to me?"

And now this.

The phone rang. *Oh, Lord, I hope it isn't Mom. I need more time to get ready.*

But when he picked up, he heard Francesca's voice. "Father, the archbishop is on the line for you."

"Yes, of course, put the call right through." It was too late to pretend he was in the chapel praying. Besides, that would only be putting off the inevitable.

"Brent, how are you today?" The archbishop's voice resounded firmly across the line, loud and clear.

"Not too bad, Your Grace, but I suppose you have heard the awful news about the, uh, event here at Saint Rita's?" *I might as well get this over with.*

"Yes, what an awful shock! I was very sorry to hear about Mr. Cambio's death. Are there any details forthcoming from the police just yet?"

Father Bunt realized he had picked up a pencil and had been mindlessly doodling on his calendar, where he had sketched a hangman's noose. Now he drew firm lines through it as he answered.

"The police so far believe that Mr. Cambio was killed by a head injury that resulted from a heavy book case, uh, falling on him. But until we have the final coroner's report, we won't know for certain. At this point, however, they are treating this as a . . . as a homicide. It seems that Mr. Cambio had quite a few . . . had made a number of . . . enemies here."

There was a deafening silence on the other end of the line. Father Bunt was well aware that there had been another homicide involving this very parish just the previous year. After what seemed like an hour, but was actually less than a minute, the archbishop spoke again.

"Well, that is very unfortunate." He pronounced the next words slowly and carefully as if they were a secret code. "Enemies. Very. Unfortunate. Indeed." Now there was a pause. "Are there any suspects at this point?"

"The police haven't mentioned any."

"Well, you keep me informed."

There was another pause as the archbishop cleared his throat. "We have our lawyers, of course, looking at all the legal ramifications. They're going to fax you some recommendations for dealing with the media fallout. The press will be all over this, Brent, and we have to proceed very cautiously."

Another throat clearing and then, "I'll put my secretary on the line and you can set up an appointment to meet with the legal department, all right?"

"Yes, sir."

After the call, Father Bunt began sketching a dog from his childhood: a golden retriever named Rover. He had been extremely adept at obeying commands.

* * * *

In the Decatur police department later that day, Tony was fielding calls from various parishioners at Saint Rita's who wanted more details about the case than they could find in the newspaper.

"Is there a killer on the loose in our parish?" one lady demanded to know. "Because I have children in the school there, and this is completely unacceptable."

When there was a break from the calls, one of the other officers who knew about the case handed Tony a cup of coffee. "Why don't you just let the answering machine pick up and take messages?"

"Then I just have to return the calls later. This way, I get things out of the way immediately."

Tony winced as he took a sip of the bitter black liquid that had probably been brewed the previous day.

"You wouldn't expect things like this to happen at a church, would you?" the other officer said and then paused. "What'd you say the name was?"

"Saint Rita's"

"Oh." Another pause. "So what's she the patron Saint of anyway?"

Tony put down the cup of coffee. "Impossible causes."

"Well, good luck, man. You're gonna need it."

* * * *

Maria held the envelope she'd discovered in her purse. She turned it over and saw that it was addressed to her, although she hadn't seen it before. *Who could have slipped this into my purse without my noticing it? And whose handwriting is this?*

Cautiously, she turned it over in her hands as if it were a grenade that might suddenly explode. The envelope was open; she extracted a single sheet of white stationery that seemed to be very good quality. She read it quickly. *Oh, Lord, I hope Paul didn't read this.*

* * * *

Glancing at the car clock, Francesca parked near the church and hurried inside. She was ten minutes late. The funeral would start at 11 a.m., but the choir was supposed to be there to rehearse no later than 9:30. And although she had pledged not to return to the choir, she had decided to make an exception, since this was a funeral Mass.

It looked like she was not alone in her sentiments, as most of the choir was there—even folks who had vowed they would never be caught dead singing contemporary hymns. The choir stumbled along during the rehearsal with the new director doing his best to lead them, although he seemed lost without Chip there.

Despite the many people whose feathers Chip had ruffled, she noticed that the turnout for the funeral was good. The people of Saint Rita's weren't the types to hold a grudge against a dead man. Father William was the celebrant that day, and he had put together a decent sermon, reminding the congregation that no man can predict the hour of his death, so we must be ready at all times.

The choir director had chosen opening and closing hymns from the blue paperback hymnal, which Francesca had heard some of the baritones call "the blue abomination."

He told the choir they would be singing "On Eagles' Wings" for the Communion hymn because the director was sure Chip would want that one. Loud sighs could be heard emanating from the tenor section.

The choir sat at the back of the church, behind parishioners who had their own reasons for avoiding proximity to the altar. Some were parents with infants who needed quick access to the exit if their little ones started wailing. Others were people planning to leave right after Communion. Among the latter group Francesca noticed a solidly built man, maybe in his forties, wearing a baseball cap and sunglasses, which he didn't take off during the entire Mass. There was something familiar about him that piqued her curiosity. She planned to talk with him right after the funeral, but by the time she'd gathered up her music, he was gone.

As she was leaving, Francesca ran into Margaret Hennessy, who had volunteered to help with the Mass. She asked Margaret if any of Chip's relatives had attended the funeral.

"He has some family in Florida," Margaret said. Her eyes assumed a troubled look. "The mother and sister were supposed to be here. I don't know what could have happened to them."

Now Margaret rummaged in her purse. "I did find this name in a drawer in Chip's office—Chuck—with a local address. Must be a friend of his. I'm going to give it to the police."

"I'll do it for you when I see Tony," Francesca said.

"Thank you, dear." Margaret handed her the crumpled piece of paper.

"Oh, one more thing," Margaret said, "before I forget. I have some letters back at the office that came for Chip during the week. I didn't have the heart to read them, but Tony might want to see them."

"I'm sure he would. I'll come by for them as soon as I can."

Francesca also spent a few minutes talking with some of the choir members. She noticed that Rebecca looked especially pained. Her eyes were swollen and red, and she was sniffling. When she got Rebecca alone, Francesca gave her a quick hug.

"It's terrible what happened, isn't it?"

Rebecca nodded and started to say something, but her words were choked off by a sob.

Something is definitely strange here. Why is Rebecca so torn apart by Chip's death?

Rebecca pulled out a raggedy Kleenex from her purse and began dabbing her eyes, which had smudges of mascara beneath them. She looked around as if to be sure they were alone.

"Can you keep a secret? A really big secret?"

Francesca nodded. *What's up with her?*

"I don't want the other Choir Chicks—or anyone for that matter—to know about this, but I can trust you." Rebecca paused to wipe another tear that had escaped from her eye and was making a smudgy stream down her cheek.

"I'm really embarrassed about this, but . . . well, I hope you'll understand. You see, I was dating Chip."

Francesca waited for more. She was well aware that "dating" could have multiple meanings, and she hoped, for Rebecca's sake, that the arrangement had been very casual and in the beginning stages.

"Was it . . . serious?" She inwardly uttered a prayer that the answer would be in the negative.

There was a very audible sigh, and then another dark tear made its way down Rebecca's cheek. "Well, not really. Let's put it this way: I thought we were seeing each other exclusively, but it soon became clear that Chip wasn't looking for anything really . . . committed. It took me a while to see the blinding light of the obvious."

Rebecca dabbed at her nose. "He is . . . was . . . a playboy. I think there are plenty of women he was dating right here at the parish."

Francesca winced. She wondered if Rebecca knew she had gone out to dinner with Chip.

Best to just tell her.

"Listen, Rebecca, I had a dinner date with him, that's all."

Rebecca frowned. "I didn't even know about that. I was referring to other women like that *Maria Grabowski.*" She spoke the name as if it were an evil incantation.

"For Heaven's sake, Rebecca—Maria is married!"

"That didn't seem to stop Chip, and apparently it didn't stop Maria either."

At that moment, the lights went out. The church had emptied, and the custodian was signaling it was time for him to clean up.

"Well, I guess that's our cue," Rebecca said. "I can't talk more now anyway. I just want to go home and get into bed. This has all been really stressful."

After Rebecca left, Francesca went to the chapel and said a Rosary for the repose of Chip's soul. She also said a few decades for Rebecca, who was obviously taking his death very hard. As she was praying, she noticed the blissful absence of music. *Father Bunt must have asked someone to disconnect the speakers.*

She then walked to her car in the largely empty parking lot. It was a lovely day, and she wished she'd walked to church. The Italian food from Benedetti's, combined with Bruster's ice cream and then lunch at the Lebanese Grill, had taken its toll: her daily weigh-in had revealed she'd gained three pounds.

When she left the church, however, her car seemed to automatically drive over to the Publix grocery store on North Decatur Road, where she hurried inside and picked up a box of vanilla ice-cream sandwiches. No matter what the scale said, she wanted comfort food. She could always diet tomorrow. She also picked up a bag of fried chicken tenders from the deli section, and then, at the last minute, to calm her conscience she added a bag of mixed salad greens. As she pulled into her driveway, she saw Bainbridge, her next-door neighbor's dog, sitting on her porch. He seemed to be waiting for her, so she fed him a chicken tender before going inside.

Entering the living room, she looked around with a critical eye. Even though she lived alone with Tubs, the place was a total mess. There were piles of books stacked by her chair, an eclectic mix of light mysteries by one of her favorite authors, M. C. Beaton, as well as what Tony jokingly called her "heavy reading" books. There was one called *Interior Freedom*, which was all about trying to live more in the present. Near the books was an empty plate with cookie crumbs, along with a few crumpled Hershey's chocolate bar wrappers. As she straightened up the books, she noticed fat dust bunnies gathering strength under her favorite chair. *When was the last time I cleaned the house?*

She remembered how Dean used to hide chocolates from her, doling them out on special occasions, because she had such a fierce sweet tooth that once a box of treats were opened, she would be tempted to eat them all at once. Now when she cleaned the house, she often unearthed hidden caches of chocolates, and then she would cry because she knew that one day she'd discover the last one. She picked up the framed photo of her and Dean on their wedding day and planted a soft kiss on his face.

After supper, she dug out the wrinkled piece of paper that Margaret Hennessy had given her. *I should give this to Tony, but why don't I check it out first?* She imagined Tony warning her to keep out of the investigation, but she also had another fantasy that started gaining strength and wiped out all the warnings. She pictured the two of them sipping champagne together. He would say, "I don't know what I'd do without you, Francesca. We're really a team. I couldn't have solved this case without your help."

The address was in Decatur, so it didn't take her long to get there. It was a condo not far from the town square. She rang the doorbell and someone came to the door quickly. As the door opened, she drew back with a feeling combining shock, fear, and nausea.

Oh, God! It's Chip!

Chapter 9

After the funeral, Maria took out the letter again. The envelope was addressed to her and had been sealed, but then it had been torn open. She also noticed that it was postmarked five days prior to Chip's death. This meant that someone had opened the letter and then held on to it before putting it in her purse so she would see it. *Paul? But I can't ask him—he'll get suspicious.*

She licked her lips nervously and read the letter again. This was a definite love letter, the old-fashioned kind that had words like "undying love" and "soul mates" liberally poured out. And even before she had seen the signature she had suspected that it was from Chip. No doubt about it: anyone who read this letter would conclude that she and Chip were having a torrid love affair. *Holy Mother of God, what should I do?*

* * * *

The words were bubbling up in Francesca's throat, but they wouldn't come out. Her heart was pounding so hard she was sure the man standing there could hear it. But the man, who couldn't possibly be Chip, seemed quite aware of her fright.

"Please, don't get upset. I know what you're thinking, but I'm not Chip. He never told you he had a twin brother, did he?"

"A bro-bro-brother?" She leaned against the door, wondering how long it would take her body to get over its automatic panic reaction.

The man's brow developed a deep furrow. "Yes, as you can see, identical, in fact." He opened the door even wider. "Why don't you come in?"

She headed into his living room, where she sank down on the couch, still shaking. "I'm Francesca, from Saint Rita's," she managed to say as he took a seat in a nearby rocking chair.

She noticed that he even dressed like his brother, in a crisp Oxford cloth shirt and carefully pressed slacks.

"I apologize for scaring you like this," he said.

Francesca finally got around to answering the man's question. "Chip never told me . . . I . . . oh, Lord, I'm confused . . ."

He picked up a bottle of wine that was on the coffee table. "Let me get you a glass of wine to calm your nerves."

He left the room, evidently in search of a glass, while she tried to compose herself. Her eyes quickly scanned the room. It was sparsely furnished, with just a couch, a rocker, and the coffee table. There were no bookshelves and no knickknacks, but on the mantel was one framed photo showing twin boys in matching suits, holding rabbits in their arms on what looked like Easter Sunday.

"White OK?" he called from the kitchen.

"Oh, yes, anything is fine."

When he came back in, he handed her a glass of wine, and she accepted it from him, avoiding his eyes and wondering if he could tell that her hands were trembling.

As she took the first sip, an image flashed through her mind. "Were you . . . were you by any chance at Chip's funeral?"

"Yes, I just had to go, but I tried to disguise myself the best I could—with that dumb baseball cap and glasses."

She nodded. "I thought I saw you there. I'm . . . I'm so sorry about your loss."

He twirled the stem of the wine glass in his hands. "Thanks. It's been a really rough ride."

* * * *

A sharp knock came at Father Bunt's door. He was composing a letter to his parents on the computer. They'd find out soon enough about the situation at Saint Rita's, and he'd rather they heard it from him first. The door opened and in came the parish secretary, Leticia O'Connor. She had been nicknamed "Mrs. O" by the children, and the adults often called her "O" for short.

O was a petite redhead in her midthirties with a smattering of freckles that Father Bunt thought gave her a little-girl look. He noticed that, right now, her freckles were standing out precipitously on her unusually pale face. She was carrying some sheets of paper.

"Father, I hate to disturb you, but I needed to check with you about some . . . expenditures."

Her tone of voice reminded him of the time his aunt had called to tell him she had cancer. He nodded at O, and she came into the room and perched on the edge of the chair in front of his desk. She cleared her throat with a little squeaking sound.

"Father, I just got our bank statement and it seems there was a large sum of money transferred from the building fund to the music account—and then transferred to an entirely different account, outside the church."

When he heard "large sum of money," he felt a quiver of fear pierce his heart.

"How large?"

Now O's face started to redden dangerously. "Two hundred thousand dollars."

"Who transferred it?"

"Well, Father, the thing is . . . I mean, the only person who has access to the building fund is . . . the . . . the pastor."

His own voice sounded odd to him, as if he were inside a barrel. "I didn't make the transfer, so someone must have gotten into my office and used the computer."

O's face grew even redder and she appeared to be shrinking in the chair. "Father, you and I have access to your office, and so does Father William—and anyone with a master key—but only *you* could get into the savings account, unless . . ." She coughed nervously.

"Unless?"

"Unless someone figured out the password."

He stood up and paced the floor, absently plunging his hands in his pockets and jingling the change. He had a meeting with the lawyers later that day and he could just imagine the expressions on their faces when he dropped this particular bomb. They'd ask him, of course, whether someone on the staff could be the culprit. He knew Father William was in the clear, and there was no way he would ever suspect O, who had been a faithful employee of the parish for ten years. What about Maria and Francesca? They had keys as well. He suddenly stopped pacing, and the jingling came to an abrupt halt. He looked out the window and spied a squirrel tentatively making its way across the street. He watched as the animal managed to dart around three cars and spring to safety on a patch of grass on the other side. He shook his head. There was no way he could reasonably suspect either of the two women.

"When did this happen?" he asked.

"The end of last month. The 28th."

He licked his lips nervously as he glanced at his calendar. *Three days before Chip was killed.*

He went over the facts in his mind. According to the police, a master key to the parish had been found in Chip's pocket when he died. This, of course, meant the man could have come into his office and accessed his computer. Now Father Bunt groaned inwardly as he realized there were times he had left his computer on when he left the office for an hour or so to grab lunch or attend a meeting.

Worse yet, he could recall times when he had been checking figures online and had left himself logged into the church's savings accounts. He knew that the system would automatically log him off after just a few minutes of inactivity, which meant the guilty party would've had only a small window of opportunity. It would have to be someone who was pretty familiar with his routines. He tried to remember the last time he had checked the balance on the building fund, but it wasn't something he did regularly.

He turned to face O. "We'll have to notify the police about this, of course. We need to figure out where the money is now, and if anyone has spent it."

"But how, Father? I mean, how could someone make the transfer?"

The squirrel was now crouched on a limb just outside his window, munching on an acorn in a carefree manner. *I never thought I'd envy the life of a squirrel.*

"Well, someone might have stolen a master key and unlocked my office . . . and got into my computer." He decided not to mention that no one would need the password, since the machine would have been conveniently left on.

O nodded and he noticed that the lines in her brow smoothed over. *The poor woman probably thought I was going to accuse her.*

He tried to smile reassuringly to allay her fears, but his lips felt dry and tense. "Don't worry, O, we'll get to the bottom of this. For now, please don't spread the word about this . . . problem."

But he could tell by the expression on her face that she already had, and the whole parish would soon be abuzz about this latest catastrophe.

* * * *

As the days wore on, the situation worsened. Father Bunt soon learned there was also money missing from some of the other accounts, including the Saint Vincent de Paul Society's. He found the latter particularly distressing; he hated to think Chip would stoop so low as to steal from the poor. Still, Judas had held the money bag for the apostles, and much of that money had gone to the poor. No doubt Judas had helped himself now and again.

But immediately he chastised himself. *Maybe I'm wrong to accuse Chip. Maybe he had nothing to do with the thefts. Maybe it was the murderer.* But Chip's illicit master key seemed to cry out loud and clear that the man had been up to no good. Besides, the huge transfer of money had gone right into that special music account, which Chip had carte blanche to write checks on.

Father Bunt walked in circles in his study. In a panic, he rummaged through his desk drawer and found Chip's résumé. His heart sank as he realized that he had not made a thorough check of the man's credentials when he hired him. After all, Chip had presented himself as the perfect candidate, above any suspicion. Besides, Father Bunt reminded himself, he had been too busy to follow up on references.

With trembling hands, he now picked up the phone and made a few calls. In minutes, he had his answers. Although Chip had indeed worked at the churches listed, he had left each one under "unfortunate circumstances." Two of the pastors didn't want to divulge the details, but the third came right out with it: "Let's just say we had some money missing from various accounts. Not a lot, you understand, but enough to raise some flags. And even though I couldn't pin the blame exactly on Cambio, my gut instinct told me he was up to no good. Besides, he was a bit of a Romeo, if you catch my drift, and he also riled up plenty of people with all the changes he was making. So I told him money was short and just let him go."

Father Bunt sat miserably at his desk, staring into space. *Chip must've been betting I'd be so charmed by his interview I wouldn't make the calls. And it looks like he won that bet.*

* * * *

Father William was at his wits' end. For one, he very much missed Father John, who had spent time with him each week, going over various snags in his sermons and advising him on everything from buying tires for his car to handling the odd situations that sometimes arose during confessions.

Father William had discovered during his first months as a priest that some people came to Confession when they were actually in need of psychiatric help, and it had been difficult to know how to direct them. There were also teenagers who came because they had been pressured by their parents. They sat there in glum silence, insisting they really had no sins to confess. He typically gave them a blessing and an examination-of-conscience pamphlet to consult before they came to him again.

There were also the overly scrupulous, most notably a group of elderly ladies from one of the nearby senior homes, who came to Confession on the bus every Saturday without fail. Father William strongly suspected that some of them were exaggerating their sinfulness, or at least he hoped so. He just couldn't bear to think that the ladies with puffy white hair and sensible shoes were engaging in some of the activities at the senior residence that they claimed they were. And if they were, he wondered why he wasn't hearing the confessions of the old men.

But all these dilemmas had to be stashed away because Father Bunt seemed too deeply troubled to have any spare time to talk these days. The pastor was either on the phone with the archbishop, answering calls from the police station, talking to lawyers from the chancery, or trying to assuage the worries of various parishioners. Even at supper, Father Bunt seemed distracted. He rarely commented any more on Maria's cooking, and the poor woman looked disheartened.

Then there was the ongoing problem of Ignatius, last sighted at the disastrous lunch with the archbishop and still on the loose. Although the scattered piles of sunflower seeds were continuing to disappear, and the little dishes of water were slowly being emptied, Father William was beginning to wonder if he would ever capture the little creature.

* * * *

Tony toyed with a rubber band at his desk. According to the coroner's report, Chip had died of a broken neck. Death had probably occurred in a matter of minutes, which at least meant he hadn't been lying there for hours in pain. Whoever had come in and pushed the shelves over had to have known that he would be there that night. There were no signs of a struggle. When the custodian had found Chip's body later that night, the door had been partially ajar.

Tony figured this meant one of two things: either Chip had left it open when he went in, or the murderer had left it open upon exiting. If the former were true, then the killer would not have had to possess a master key, though he would have to have known about Chip's whereabouts that night. So who would have known that? Here Tony extracted a stick of gum from his desk drawer and chewed it thoughtfully. *Chip could have told any number of people that he'd be in the library working late that night.*

Tony had also heard from the thoroughly rattled Father Bunt, who had filled him in on details about the big money transfer at the parish. Bunt said there were also items that had been discovered missing after Chip's death—some pricey gold chalices, crucifixes, and candlesticks. Chip certainly looked like the culprit, but Tony had been in homicide long enough to avoid drawing conclusions too quickly. There could be a thief on the loose in the parish, someone with no connection to Chip. Here Tony massaged his forehead as he felt the first signs of a headache. *Stealing from the altar. How low can you go?*

Tony got up and poured himself a cup of coffee from the communal pot, which seemed to always be about half full. As he sipped the acrid liquid, he continued pondering the case. Assuming that Chip was the thief, why hadn't he hightailed it out of town right after he stole the money? Why hang around to pack up the hymnals? Of course, Chip was smart enough to realize the bank statement wouldn't show up for a while, but he was taking a chance that Bunt might check the balance. Tony added some powdered creamer to the coffee. Maybe Chip was a weird sort of perfectionist, and he didn't want to leave the parish until he got rid of the old hymnals once and for all. Tony shook his head, thinking of all the strange cases he'd investigated over the years. *This one could make the top ten.*

CHAPTER 10

Francesca was at her desk in the rectory, trying to keep her mind on answering the phone and fielding questions from parishioners. She still didn't know what she should do about Chip's brother. They had talked for about two hours, and he had really opened up to her. He had told her quite candidly what life had been like as an identical twin to someone whose values he did not share.

"We were diametrically opposed on just about everything, even if we looked alike." Chuck had rocked miserably in the chair as he sipped his wine and told her his story.

"When we were growing up, if he sneezed, I was sure to follow a second later. We never had separate rooms, separate wardrobes, separate teachers at school. He was like my shadow."

Here he had paused to undo the top button of his shirt, as if the memory were strangling him. "We went our different ways, finally, after college. He was big on the contemporary music scene and started to carve out a niche for himself as a liturgist. As for me, I couldn't stand the tacky changes he foisted onto parishes."

"Was Chip actually Catholic?" It was a question that had been preying on her mind for some time.

"Well, it depends on your definition. It's like a lot of the politicians you read about. He didn't agree with many Church teachings, but he still went to Mass and all—and he definitely claimed the title."

"And you?"

"Like I said, he and I were polar opposites. My only bone of contention with the Church is some of the music that's allowed at Mass. I like traditional hymns, the organ, and the Gregorian chants—which I've studied a little."

At that moment, she had realized where Chip had gotten that Gregorian chant tape that he played in his car the night she went out with him.

"Chuck, do you have any idea who could have killed your brother? Did he have any enemies from his past?"

"Not really, unless you count all the people who wanted to throttle him over the music and stuff."

He had stood up and begun pacing the room. "I'm really glad you came to see me. I want to find the killer, and, frankly, I don't trust the police to do the job right."

"Why not?"

"From what I've heard, Chip stirred up a big hornet's nest at Saint Rita's. The police aren't going to go out of their way trying to clear his name—and I doubt anyone will insist they do. I've already heard rumors that Chip is being blamed for all sorts of things at the parish." He paused. "Like some missing money."

At this point, Chuck had pulled his chair nearer to her and stared earnestly into her eyes. Although he looked eerily like his brother, there was something about his eyes that seemed steadier.

"My brother had all kinds of faults, but he was still my brother. And even if he had terrible taste in liturgy, he was basically a good guy. I want to get to the bottom of what's going on at the parish." There had been a pleading look in the eyes, and he had seemed to be tearing up.

"I'm sure you understand, Francesca. I don't want everything blamed on him. I know he wasn't a thief."

She had agreed to keep Chuck's identity a secret, but now she felt guilty because this meant withholding from Tony what could be important information. Her plan had been to help Tony with the case, but she hadn't banked on Chuck extracting a promise of secrecy from her. *Oh, why does life have to be so complicated?* But Chuck had pleaded with her, and she didn't think it would do any harm to go along with his secret, at least for a while.

Chuck had assured her that he would eventually let Father Bunt and the police know about his identity. He wanted time to do some investigating on his own. She just hoped he didn't give anyone else the same scare he'd given her.

* * * *

Maria was in the kitchen alone, cleaning up after lunch. Francesca had just left and the afternoon volunteer had called in sick, which meant the answering machine would be picking up the calls. As she sponged down the table, she felt her eyes stinging with tears. There were a lot of leftovers these days because both priests seemed distracted and worried, and their appetites weren't what they used to be.

In the old days, before the murder, the priests had usually wanted seconds, and there had been times when she had almost run out of food. Now she mournfully spooned the mashed potatoes into a Tupperware container and wrapped the still-warm biscuits carefully in foil. She felt a lump in her throat when she noticed there were two pork chops left over.

Just then, she heard the kitchen door nudge its way open, and in came Dopey. She couldn't help but feel better when she looked at him. He had recently consumed an extra large can of dog food, but she could tell by the gleam in his eyes that he would probably like a pork chop as well. Usually she didn't give Dopey meat from the table because he was, as Father Bunt was constantly reminding her, only a dog. But today she made an exception. The dog tore the meat from the two chops quickly and then ran off with a greasy bone in his mouth. *I hope he doesn't bury it in the couch.* She recalled how Father Bunt had nearly had a fit when he'd discovered five dog biscuits and a smelly rawhide bone in the recesses of his favorite chair. *Bless his heart.*

She busied herself filling the dishwasher and sweeping the floor, while mentally trying to figure out what to do about the letter from Chip. *Should I bring it up with Paul or just keep my mouth shut until he mentions it? Maybe it will all blow over.*

She walked down the hallway and noticed that the door to Chip's office was open. *I guess the custodian forgot to lock it.* She went over and began to close the door. But then she looked inside and saw someone rummaging through the drawers of the desk. The man looked up, quite startled, and Maria shrieked. *Chip's ghost!* She turned away quickly and that was all she remembered.

* * * *

A few moments later, Father Bunt came downstairs to get a glass of iced tea. Maria wasn't in the kitchen, but the electric range was on, so he figured she had left for a moment. He thought he heard something in the hall, so he walked out of the kitchen and looked down the hall. He spotted Maria lying crumpled on the floor.

"Dear God, now what?" He rushed over, bent down, and felt for her pulse. Then he called out her name loudly, over and over. In a few seconds, she opened her eyes and looked at him with a confused and frightened expression.

He patted her hand nervously. "Are you alright, my dear? What happened?"

She sat up slowly. "Oh, Father, I had a terrible fright. I saw something . . . I just can't . . ."

"Take your time, and don't be afraid. Now, what did you see?"

Maria managed to get to her feet, and he helped her to a chair in the kitchen. Her hair was awry and her blue eye shadow had smudged, so she looked as if someone had hit her.

Her voice was only a whisper. "Father, I saw a ghost. I saw Chip's ghost!"

He poured her a glass of tea. "Here, drink this, it will help you."

She emptied the glass like an obedient child, but then looked at him as if seeing him for the first time. "Father, I tell you, it was Chip! Right there in his office!"

He pulled up a chair and sat down beside her. "Now, Maria, you know there are no such things as ghosts. Chip—may he rest in peace—is either in Heaven, Hell, or Purgatory." *Probably Hell.*

"But Father . . ."

"Maria, look, you've been working too hard. This whole terrible event has taken its toll on all of us. Why don't you take the rest of the day off? Go home and get some rest."

"Yes, Father, but I know what I saw." And with that, she had rinsed out the iced tea glass, picked up her voluminous purse, and departed for the day.

After she had gone home, Father Bunt prayed an extra Rosary for poor Maria, who seemed to be having some sort of breakdown. *The wheels are really coming off this place.*

Everyone was gone from the rectory, even Father William, who was having supper at a parishioner's home. The only living creatures at home were himself, that stupid dog, and the hamster—who, thank God, had been found safe and sound, Maria had told him, and was back in the cage. *That had better be the truth.*

Father Bunt settled into his chair, relishing a few moments of solitude. He fished around in the cushions to find the little prayer book he had been reading there the night before. Then he withdrew his hand in horror. A greasy pork chop bone had been hidden beneath the cushion.

* * * *

Maria's mother met her at the front door of her house. Her eyes were red and puffy.

"Momma! What's wrong?"

"It's Paul. The police came and took him for questioning."

"Momma, what do you mean? Why?"

The old lady twisted her handkerchief nervously and dabbed at her streaming eyes. "They said something about a murder at the church. Maria, what has Paul done?"

Maria felt her heart rate quicken in fear. She sat down heavily on the couch. "Nothing, Momma, nothing. I'm sure it's just routine."

* * * *

Tony drove by Francesca's late that night. *I'll only ring the bell if her lights are on.* He was relieved to see that they were.

"Tony, come in! It's so good to see you!" She gave him a quick hug, but he noticed her eyes looked troubled.

"What's wrong, Francesca? You seem worried."

"Oh, Tony, it's nothing. Maybe it's just all the stress about Chip's death and everything . . ."

"Are you sure there isn't something else bothering you?"

She looked down at her feet. "Really, no, everything's fine. Come on in and have a glass of wine."

Tony took off his jacket and threw it over a nearby chair. "I can't stay long. I just came by to tell you about Paul."

"Did something happen to Paul?"

He took her hand and gave it a gentle squeeze. "Paul is fine. Nothing has happened to him. We're just questioning him about Chip's death."

Her forehead furrowed in worry. "Oh, God, poor Maria! Do you really think Paul did it?" She sat down on the couch.

Tony didn't want to worry her even more, but he knew she'd find out eventually. "Look, Francesca, this is all in confidence at this point, but as much as I hate to say this, I really think we have the right guy."

She picked up a paper towel from the coffee table and began pleating it nervously. "But Tony, he's such a nice man! A family man! Why would he do something like this?"

Tony sat down beside her. "Maybe I'll take that glass of wine after all."

She poured them both generous glasses and then sat back down on the couch.

"Francesca, it seems Chip was coming on to Maria. Making moves—you know. And jealousy can be a very strong motive for crimes. Men don't always act rationally when their wives are fooling around."

"I just can't believe that Maria and Chip . . . it doesn't make sense."

"Well, not much about murder cases ever does. And I'm sorry for upsetting you. But I wanted you to know before rumors start spreading."

She put her wine glass down. "But he's innocent until proven otherwise, right?" She looked so hopeful, he had to reassure her.

"That's right, so don't worry. The truth will come out."

Her cheeks had flushed slightly. "I hope so." Then she refilled their glasses. "Tony, please tell me—why are you so sure it's Paul?"

"Well, we decided to question anyone with a master key to the library to see if they had an alibi. The priests are in the clear. They were having supper at a parishioner's house.

She shifted on the couch. "But I have a key, too, Tony."

He smiled. "That's right. But you were out with me that night, so you're completely and entirely off the hook. The parish secretary was at a neighbor's open house. The custodian was out of town, and didn't return until later that night. That left Maria. And we found out she'd been at the movies with a friend, and they went out for dessert afterward. Her mother had taken the children to visit their aunt for an overnight stay. Paul claimed he was home alone all evening, but he had no way to prove he didn't take a quick trip over to Saint Rita's."

"But didn't Maria have the master key with her?"

"She didn't take it with her that night, and Paul knew where she kept it in the house."

"What time did the crime actually happen, Tony?"

"Coroner's report says between 9 and 11 p.m. And Maria and her friend were out until midnight."

There was a plaintive meow. Francesca looked down and saw Tubs staring at her, and then she helped him onto the couch. "Isn't all this . . . what's the word . . . circumstantial evidence?"

"Well, Paul also admitted he suspected his wife was fooling around with Chip. Evidently he had found a love letter."

"But how would Paul have known Chip would be in the library that night?"

"He didn't have to. My guess is he wanted to warn Chip to stay away from his wife. He probably went by Chip's house first, saw the car wasn't there, and then went to the church. Once he was there, he must have seen the lights on in the library."

She sighed heavily. "But he hasn't confessed to any of this, right?"

"No, he claims he was home all evening, but there's no one who can vouch for his alibi. He admitted he was drinking that night. And in my opinion, that might explain why he did something that seems very much out of character for him."

Francesca stroked Tubs under the chin, while he purred furiously. "Tony, I hate to even think this, but what about the nuns? Do any of them have a key?"

"No, and believe me, I'm relieved. I sure didn't want to cross-examine the good sisters!"

He decided not to share his theory that the door could have been left ajar by Chip, in which case the master key was irrelevant. *After all, Chip was doing something secretive, and it's highly likely he had locked the door behind him—in which case, Paul really is our man.* He wanted to discourage Francesca from getting involved in the investigations, so he gave her a look that he hoped would convey the seriousness of his words.

"Look, Francesca, don't start playing detective, OK? You know how dangerous that can be, right?"

"I know, Tony, but it's . . . it's just in my nature to wonder. I mean, I have trouble just sitting back and letting things unfold. I seem to have this . . . I don't know what to call it . . . urge, I guess . . . to investigate."

"Maybe you missed your calling," he said wryly. "Instead of that psychology minor in college, maybe you should have gone into police work."

"We both know that's a real laugh. I mean, I'll admit I have a curious mind, but I hate danger."

He moved closer to her. "You know what? I think you should leave it all to me. This is what they pay me for, after all—to find the bad guys."

She knew she should confess to him what she had been up to. *I should tell him about Chuck, but I know he'd get angry with me.*

"I guess you're right, but . . . ," she started to say, but he interrupted her by leaning in and kissing her fully on the lips.

She felt herself responding. She yearned to relax into the sweetness of the kiss, and just let herself go, but something stopped her. They had kissed before, but never so intensely. She could sense real passion in him, and it scared her.

He pulled back. "What is it, Francesca? You don't seem . . . all here."

"Maybe I'm not." She stood up and walked across the room and glanced at the wedding photo.

"It's Dean, isn't it? You're thinking about him, right?"

"Yes, guilty as charged." She adjusted the photo. "For some reason, he's really on my mind tonight."

Tony felt a bitter wave of something rise in his throat, and was horrified to realize it was jealousy. *How can I be jealous of a dead man?* But there it was, and before he could stop himself he said something he later would regret.

"I can't compete with him, Francesca. It's impossible."

"What do you mean?" Her face was reddening.

He could feel his heart thudding heavily in his chest. "Well, for the love of God, he's a Saint, isn't he? I mean, everything you've told me about him makes me sure he was perfect. And let's face it, I'm far from perfect." He stood up and picked up his jacket from the nearby chair. Tubs jumped off the couch, as if sensing the sudden change of mood in the room.

"Tony, please tell me you're not jealous of Dean!"

"Francesca, look around you. You have six photos of Dean in this one room alone. You've turned the place into a shrine! When are you going to let go?"

Now I've done it, he thought, as he saw her lips trembling.

"Never—that's when. Please, Tony, I think you should leave."

He didn't want to leave, but he could tell there was no way out of this one. "You got it!"

And with that he was gone.

* * * *

What a disaster. Francesca rolled over in bed and thought about the previous night. How had things gone downhill so quickly? Why had Tony lost his temper like that? And was he right? Was she turning Dean into a Saint, into an impossible ideal that no living man could compete with?

She looked up at the dresser and saw three framed photos of her and Dean. She looked at the bedside table. There was a group shot of her aunts and uncles and cousins at a reunion five years before—and, of course, there was Dean smiling up at the camera, his arm wrapped protectively around her shoulder. *Oh, Lord, maybe Tony is right.*

She glanced over and saw Tubs stretched out next to her. At that precise moment, his big, slanted, yellow-green eyes opened and he began to purr. He gazed at her with what looked like interest, although she figured he was just hungry. *Is this how I'm going to live the rest of my life, sleeping with a cat?* She sighed heavily and climbed out of bed. She wanted to call Tony, but she also felt he had been out of line. *He should apologize first, and then I will.*

She arrived at Saint Rita's an hour early so she could pray in the little chapel. She smiled when she remembered the days when Dean had been alive and how she would tell him she was going out for a while, and he would ask where, and she would say, "To see Jesus." He always said, "Tell Him hello for me."

And she always had prayed for her beloved husband, every morning and every night. Still, she thought, as she sat there, looking at the tender morning light awakening colors in the stained-glass windows, despite her prayers, he had been killed. *Maybe Tony's right. Maybe I'm too wrapped up in memories.*

At that moment, she heard the door to the chapel open, and she turned to see Maria hurrying in, looking harried and upset. Maria sat down next to her in the pew. They were alone in the chapel.

"I hate to disturb you; please forgive me," Maria whispered, "but I saw your car outside and I had to talk to you. Something terrible has happened."

Francesca didn't want to tell Maria that she already knew about Paul's arrest, so she remained silent. Maria sat hunched over in the pew, wrapping her arms around her chest, but she never mentioned Paul. Instead, she told Francesca in a breathless and nervous voice that she had seen Chip's ghost.

"I don't care what Father Bunt says about how ghosts don't exist. He's got it all wrong. I'm telling you, as sure as I'm sittin' in this chapel, I saw Chip's ghost in his office."

Now what? I know who it was, but I'm sworn to secrecy.

Francesca was just about to assure Maria that ghosts didn't exist when the chapel door opened again and in came Father William, who genuflected, nodded briefly at them, went into one of the pews, and bowed his head in prayer. Maria took that as her cue to leave.

Chapter 11

Father Bunt picked up the ringing phone in his office and heard Francesca's voice: "It's the archbishop, Father."

Was it his imagination, or did her voice have an unusually nervous edge to it?

"Yes, put him through then."

Her volume dropped a bit. "Uh, Father, he's actually here, downstairs, and he wants to see you."

Father Bunt felt his heart give an odd lurch, the same way it had in elementary school when he'd been called to the blackboard to do an arithmetic problem in front of the whole class. Invariably, he would cause the chalk to squeak, and the kids would shriek with laughter. Later, the bullies would torment him because he was much thinner than the rest of the boys, and they called him "toothpick arms" in gym class.

"Father? Are you there?"

He realized he was flexing a bicep muscle. "Yes, send him right up."

In a panic, he tried to bring some order to his desk. Ordinarily, everything was in neat piles and each pencil was precisely sharpened because he liked things to be clean and tidy, but in the past week, it seemed that everything had fallen into chaos.

He brushed off his shirt, noticing that there were off-white hairs clinging to the black fabric from that stupid, mangy dog, while simultaneously rushing across the room to open the door for the archbishop, who seemed to have gotten up the stairs at lightning speed.

Father Bunt soon realized that the man, usually a jovial sort, was not in a very good humor.

"Brent, this is an unofficial visit." He sat down opposite Father Bunt.

"In matters like these with . . . criminal charges, the archdiocese has to send in the lawyers, get all the Ts crossed and Is dotted. I know you've consulted with them already, but I wanted to talk with you one-on-one."

The archbishop crossed his legs, and Father Bunt noticed that his leather shoes were immaculate and shimmered with the deep, rich gloss of black olives. He realized that he himself was wearing old jogging shoes because he had not been expecting visitors.

"I'm going to get right to the point," MacPherson announced. "The newspapers are having a field day with all the goings-on at this parish. There's the murder, for starters, but also rumors that this man you hired, this Mr. Cambio, this liturgist, was evidently fooling around with some of the women in the parish." There was an icy pause. "Married as well as unmarried."

Father Bunt opened his mouth to make a comment, but the archbishop held up his hand. The nails, Father Bunt noticed, were meticulously trimmed. The archbishop now paused to clear his throat loudly before uttering the words that Father Bunt had deeply dreaded hearing.

"Not only that, but I've learned that there are *sums of money* missing." The words shot from his mouth like little missiles.

The archbishop noticed a dog hair on his black suit jacket and flicked it off, while Father Bunt cursed the day he had allowed Maria to keep Dopey. Father Bunt started to reply, but again the archbishop indicated that he wasn't through speaking.

"Very *large* sums, I might add."

The archbishop was "using italics," something Father Bunt had always dreaded in his own father's speech habits. Father Bunt wet his lips nervously and fished for the rosary beads in his pocket.

"I know it all looks very bad right now, sir, but the police have assured me they will get to the bottom of this and find the person responsible for . . ."

MacPherson cut him off. "That is only one of my concerns, Brent. I have come here on a very different mission." He now stood up and leaned over the desk, so close that Father Bunt could see a gleaming silver nose hair that needed clipping.

"What I want to know is why in the world did you ever hire . . . a . . . *liturgist* . . . in the first place?"

Dear God, what can I say? "Your Grace, I felt the parish needed someone with experience in Church music, the liturgy, all the day-to-day details of the Mass, that is, and I wanted an expert, someone who would give his full attention to . . ."

"An *expert*?"

The word seemed suspended in the air with icicles dripping off it. "Brent, I have done some investigation into this . . . *expert* . . . you hired, and it seems that he had quite a shady track record in Florida. It looks like you hired a real scam artist and a *Romeo* to boot." He paused and drummed his fingers rapidly on the desk. "*And* a thief."

Father Bunt stalled for time by straightening out a stray paper clip on his desk. What could he really say in his own defense? Wasn't everything the archbishop said the truth?

The archbishop returned to his chair and sat down with an audible sigh. "Let me speak plainly. You did not need a liturgist. In fact, no parish needs a *lay person* telling the *pastor* how to run things. Blast it, man, *you're* the one who is supposed to be calling the shots here. *You're* supposed to be the expert! *You're* the one who is accountable before *God* for what goes on in your parish."

The archbishop pulled out his handkerchief and blew his nose in a determined fashion. "Brent, surely you must have known there were plenty of people who were opposed to the changes that were going on here. You know the difference between a liturgist and a terrorist?"

This was not the time to interrupt the archbishop, Father Bunt decided, so he tried to look as interested as possible in the punch line. Just then there was a knock at the door, and Maria came in, carrying a tray with a pot of tea, two mugs, and a big platter of chocolate-chip cookies, which were Father Bunt's favorites. The archbishop greeted her, but his lips twitched with disapproval.

"I thought y'all would like some refreshments," she said.

The archbishop smiled in a frozen way as Father Bunt made room on the little table by his desk.

She put down the tray and then left. As soon as she was gone, the archbishop fired off another question. "Isn't that the woman whose *husband* is accused of murdering the liturgist?"

"Uh, yes, that is correct. He is currently a . . . er . . . suspect."

The archbishop looked darkly at the plate of cookies. "And how do you know that *she* isn't in cahoots with her husband? If I were you, I'd be worried about what's in my soup at night."

Father Bunt had been in the process of passing the plate of cookies to the archbishop, but now he stopped in midair. MacPherson shook his head vehemently, as if the plate harbored a nest of vipers.

Father Bunt decided it would be pointless to try to defend Maria. It might just rile up MacPherson even more. Although Father Bunt didn't suspect Maria of any nefarious activity, the edge had definitely been taken off his appetite. He munched morosely on a cookie, noting she had added extra pecans and vanilla, just the way he liked. As he was trying to figure out what to say next, the archbishop suddenly rose from his chair and nearly knocked over the small end table.

"What is it, Your Grace?"

MacPherson was gesturing excitedly at something behind Father Bunt's back. "Are you aware that you have *mice* in the rectory?"

Without even turning around to see where the archbishop was looking, Father Bunt smiled.

"Not to worry, Your Grace. That's Ignatius, Father William's hamster. He gets out once in a while, but he's completely harmless."

The archbishop's face now turned a shade slightly redder than a raw New York strip steak, as he continued pointing to a spot behind Father Bunt.

"I think I know a mouse when I see one!"

Father Bunt turned around quickly. Much to his horror, he saw a creature scurrying behind his Bible. It was gray with a long, hairless tail. It was definitely not Ignatius.

* * * *

Downstairs, Francesca heard a commotion coming from Father Bunt's office and then the archbishop shouting, "For Heaven's sake, man, you need an exterminator!" Then she heard the door slamming and the sound of the archbishop hurrying down the stairs and out the front door. *Poor Father Bunt. More trouble.*

The phone rang. It was the usual drill: people who wanted the Mass and Confession schedules; an elderly woman inquiring about a bus to pick her up for Mass; a young mother with a baby screaming in the background, calling to schedule a Baptism: "This kid needs a blessing, and fast."

When there was a lull, Francesca turned over the list of suspects in her mind. No matter what Tony said, she simply couldn't believe Maria's husband was the culprit. Tony obviously thought he had the right man, but her deepest instinct said he was wrong.

She had met Paul numerous times. He was heavy set and reminded her of a bear. But although he acted rather possessively toward Maria, he seemed harmless enough. She also knew, from Maria's many stories, that the man dearly loved his four children. *Would he jeopardize everything he cared about just because he thought Maria was two-timing him?* Another voice in her head chimed in: *That's why they call some murders "crimes of passion." People do weird things when they're jealous.*

The thought of jealousy brought to mind the last time she had seen Tony. She was still miffed about that whole evening. He hadn't called since, and she was beginning to suspect he wouldn't. She missed seeing him, especially now that the investigation was in full swing. Maybe she was patting herself on the back, but when they discussed his cases, she sometimes felt she gave him a fresh perspective. She knew she should leave the investigation to him, but the possibility that the police had the wrong man, coupled with the image of the four children without their father, was too much to bear.

She took out a sheet of paper and began listing the people who might have had a particularly strong grudge against Chip. There was Sister Therese, whom he had riled a number of times. Tony had said that Sister knew about Chip's deceitful plan to ditch the hymnals, and maybe she had caught him somehow dipping his hand in the church coffers as well. Tony also had said she didn't have access to the master key, but how could he be sure? Anyone could steal a key for a few hours and make a copy.

But why kill *Chip? All Sister had to do, really, was report him to Father Bunt. However,* said another voice in her head, *maybe she figured Father wouldn't do anything. Besides, the murder could have been a spontaneous act—an angry impulse.* She recalled the day she'd met Sister outside the chapel, and how angry she'd looked.

She turned her thoughts to other potential suspects. Could a failed romance have played a role in Chip's death? She knew Rebecca had been going out with Chip, and Rebecca seemed very jealous of Maria.

She hated to put either of the women on her suspect list. After all, Rebecca was a dear friend and a meek soul, the kind of person who moved worms off the sidewalk after it rained so they wouldn't drown. Surely she was incapable of murder. And then Francesca felt a clenching in her stomach as she remembered Rebecca's outburst after the funeral. *And Rebecca teaches at Saint Rita's. Could she have stolen a master key from someone?*

Did Tony question Rebecca? She didn't recall him saying that he had.

Then there was Maria. Francesca was reluctant to admit it, but in many ways Maria was a more likely suspect than Rebecca. After all, Maria was married and perhaps she had feared that Chip would reveal his feelings to her husband—and get her in trouble. But could the motive have been something else, like jealousy on Maria's part? What if Maria had really fallen for Chip? What if they had actually been having an affair? If so, she might have been upset to discover that Chip also was seeing Rebecca—and probably other women, too. *Could she have been jealous enough to kill him?* Maria was a robust woman, and although usually rather sweet, her moods could be unpredictable. Reluctantly, Francesca put a circle around Maria's name.

Tony had said Maria was in the clear because she was at the movies that night with a friend. *But what if the friend had lied for her? Isn't that possible?* Then Francesca remembered all the philosophy courses she'd taken in college. She had learned to question every assumption, but often in real life that habit just confused her. *Am I doing that now—analyzing things too much? After all, Tony hadn't spun out an elaborate list of "what ifs" when it came to Maria.*

An image suddenly flashed in her mind. It was Mrs. Reedley from the Golden Glories club. The few times Francesca had run into the older woman, it had been very clear that she strongly disapproved of Chip's plans for the parish. *But enough to kill him?* And then there was the matter of the key again. How would Mrs. Reedley have gotten into the school library that night without it? *Ah, but what if Chip had left the door open? Then no one would need a key. Oh, Lord, more what ifs!* Although she doubted Mrs. Reedley was strong enough to have done the heinous deed, she kept her name on the list anyway. After all, she could have had an accomplice. There were plenty of people at Saint Rita's who were steamed over Chip.

The next day, Francesca was answering phones in the rectory when a very interesting call came in. It was from a woman named Garnys Feeny, who said she wanted to talk to the pastor because she had some information on the case. Father Bunt was out, and Francesca knew she should direct the woman to call Tony, but she couldn't help asking a few questions.

The woman was very talkative, and before she could stop herself, Francesca told her that she was helping the police with the investigation. Mrs. Feeny agreed to see her. *Great. Now I'm turning into a first-class liar*, Francesca thought as she hung up the phone. *But it's for a good cause. I'll just get some information from this lady and figure out if she's on the level. It'll save Tony some time—and give me an excuse to call him. I really miss him.*

After her shift was over, Francesca drove over to Ridgecrest Road in Atlanta, where the woman lived on the top floor of a large house that looked about 50 years old. In the disheveled yard strewn with shaggy piles of leaves, there was a large sheep dog, which came running toward Francesca as she walked around to the side door. Frightened, she drew back, and then heard a window open and someone downstairs call out, "Sugar Pie!" The dog bounded away, much to Francesca's relief.

She opened the side door and headed up the stairs. At the landing, she knocked on the door, which had a little sign reading, "Flowers are God's way of smiling at us." The woman who opened the door was short and bosomy, maybe 80, with frizzy, shockingly red dyed hair. Her face was heavily coated in makeup, and she peered at Francesca through thick, smudged glasses. She was wearing a Kelly-green velour running suit and white running shoes.

"You must be Francesca." She stretched out a wrinkled hand with long fingernails painted lavender. "I'm Garnys Feeny. Come on in, honey, and make yourself at home."

She led the way into a living room with two overstuffed armchairs and a sagging couch covered in a faded quilt. Pots of plastic flowers adorned the mantle, and in the corner of the room was a bird cage with a single, sky-blue parakeet in it.

The woman evidently noticed Francesca's glance. "That's Eustis. He bites, so be careful."

Then she added, "I just made some sweet tea. Can I get you a glass?"

"Oh, no, I'm fine." Francesca sank down into one of the armchairs. The woman lowered herself slowly onto the couch with a little groan—"My arthritis, honey. Don't get old!"—and then began fishing around in a nearby purse for something. She eventually located a package of Lifesavers.

"I just quit smoking last week, and I'm trying to stay on the wagon by eating candies. So far, I bet I've gained about ten pounds." She waved the package in Francesca's direction. "Want one?"

Francesca declined and waited patiently for Mrs. Feeny to extract the candy, place it in her mouth, and return the package to her purse.

With the candy in her mouth, Mrs. Feeny began her story. "I've lived in Atlanta all my life. My Horace, that's my husband, died five years ago, and that's when I sold the house and rented this apartment. You know, sugar, I sure miss him. He drank too much and sometimes he got his tail in a crack with the law, but he was a good father and provider—God rest his soul."

The air in the apartment was stifling, a mixture of old pot roast and some very flowery, sweet cologne. Francesca decided to cut to the chase. "Mrs. Feeny, I understand you might have some information about the murder case?"

The old lady sniffed loudly, and the bird let out a tentative chirp. "I believe I do. You see, I live across the street from Paul and Maria. I heard he's being questioned for . . . what do they say in the movies? Knocking the victim off?"

Francesca smiled. "Yes, I think that's it."

"Well, he couldn'tve done it, you see." There was a loud crunching sound as the candy was obliterated in the old lady's mouth.

"Do you like birds?" she suddenly asked Francesca.

"Oh, yes, I had a parakeet when I was a child." *Where is she going with this?*

"Well, I love them, and I don't just mean parakeets either. I've been a bird watcher for about 50 years. Horace and me used to go up Stone Mountain to see birds and write down the new ones. Mockingbirds, jays, wrens, towhees, hummingbirds, hawks . . ."

Francesca glanced at her watch. *Surely she isn't going to name every bird she's spotted for the past half century.*

"Robins, wrens, oh I said that already, bluebirds, doves . . . well, you get the idea. Well, those days are over. I can't climb the mountain at my age, so I use my binoculars and look for birds on my street. You'd be amazed at what I see."

Please don't start listing them again. Francesca felt her eyes watering from the stale air, but Mrs. Feeny seemed oblivious.

"You see, sometimes when I'm looking for birds, I . . . uh . . . accidentally, of course . . . might see one of my neighbors." Here Mrs. Feeny paused for a delicate cough, and Francesca noticed a little trail of red seeping into her heavily powdered cheeks.

"The night of the murder, I was looking around to see if there were any owls out, and I happened to see Paul over in his house. He was drinking beer and watching television in the living room."

"What time was that, Mrs. Feeny?"

"You call me Garnys, honey. Well, it was nine o'clock when I first noticed him, but I kept looking for owls on and off until midnight, and he never left the couch."

Francesca took out a little notebook and jotted down the times. She wanted to appear as if she were really a police assistant.

"Mrs. . . . uh . . . Garnys . . . would you be willing to swear to your testimony?"

The old lady licked her lips nervously. "I don't believe in swearing. Horace did some of that, but I told him the Lord would get him for it."

Francesca desperately wanted to laugh and tried to think about anything that would stop her, including nuclear annihilation, suicide bombings in the Middle East, and the decline in the polar bear population.

"All you have to do is sign an affidavit stating you saw Paul in his home the night of the murder. That's all."

"Do I sign it now?"

"No, at the police station." Francesca pulled out a slip of paper from her purse. "Here, I'll write down Tony Viscardi's number—he's the investigator assigned to the case—and you can set something up."

The old lady nodded, and took the piece of paper. "I just want to see justice done. That's all, honey."

Suddenly there was a piercing wolf whistle and a loud cry: "You're a red-hot momma!"

Francesca jumped, but Mrs. Feeny smiled fondly.

"Don't worry, honey, that's just Eustis. My Horace trained him."

* * * *

Tony got the call the next day. "I'm Mrs. Garnys Feeny, and I talked to your assistant . . . that pretty girl whatshername . . . Francesca . . . yes, that's it . . . yesterday about the murder case."

Tony rubbed his temples. *What the hell is Francesca up to now?*

"Yes, Mrs. Feeny, how can I help you?"

"Well, she said I should come in and see you and sign something. You see, I can clear Paul's name."

Tony gripped the phone more tightly. This could be important evidence, and he hoped Francesca hadn't compromised it.

"Great, why don't you come in and we'll talk?" After giving her directions and setting up an appointment, he dialed Francesca's home phone number. He was angry and he knew it was a bad idea to call her in this frame of mind, but he had to warn her to back off. He got her voice mail, and then he did something else he knew was always a bad idea: instead of hanging up and calling back when he was calmer, he left a message.

"I know you mean well, but PLEASE stay out of this case. I'm talking with this Feeny person tomorrow. You shouldn't have questioned her—you know that! Look, Francesca, just send any potential witnesses to me from now on, all right?"

And then he paused, trying to think of some way to soften the message, but the machine let out a bleat and his time was up. He considered calling her cell phone, but was already late for a meeting. *The damage is done.*

* * * *

Francesca was miffed when she checked her messages. *The nerve of him, talking to me that way. As if I were a child or something. I was only trying to help.*

But she felt an odd sense of unease that made it hard to justify her actions to herself. She knew she was out of line. *Did I really expect Tony to thank me for helping him? To say he was so grateful that he wanted to take me out for supper to celebrate?*

She frowned, realizing that she had just perfectly summed up exactly what she had hoped for. *And now things are just worse between us.*

Francesca decided to have a quiet evening at home. She had been invited by Molly Flowers to see a movie and have a late supper afterward, but she was yearning for a long, hot bubble bath and then a cozy evening reading a book with Tubs nestled against her. The brutal heat of summer had finally dwindled, and now the days were ever so slowly growing shorter. This meant that Halloween was around the corner, Thanksgiving was edging its way nearer, and Christmas catalogs were arriving in the mail. She felt a little blue as she ran the water for the bath.

There had been a time, when Dean was alive, when she had loved Christmas because they spent it with her cousins and her aunt in Seffner, Florida. Her other cousins from Miami would drive up to join them. On Christmas Eve there was a gigantic Italian seafood feast with everyone crowded around the table, laughing, talking, and drinking wine. Her cousin Julia would start making calzones about a month before Christmas and freezing them, and on Christmas Day, she and her husband hosted an open house for family and friends and gave them as gifts.

After Dean's death, though, holidays became days to get through, one way or the other. All the partying, the gaiety, the presents, and the feasting left Francesca feeling sad. Now, she pictured the Christmas train speeding down the tracks in her direction, loaded with gaily wrapped packages but missing the one person she wanted to spend the day with. *I could have spent it with Tony, but I'll probably never even see him again.* Pushing the dark thoughts out of her mind, she undressed and slid into the steamy, fragrant bath, watching the translucent bubbles dancing on her arms.

She had poured herself a glass of Chianti and perched it on the side of the tub. She felt her muscles letting go of their usual tension. Tubs sat nearby on the bath mat, dozing. She knew he was waiting patiently for her to make her way to the kitchen to feed him.

As she took a sip of the spicy, blood-red wine, she let her mind drift back to the murder. The one person she had not placed on her list of suspects was Chuck. It was hard to envision a brother killing his twin, but Chuck had plenty of complaints about Chip, and it sounded like he had spent a lifetime butting heads with him. *And what was he doing over at Chip's office the other day anyway? Was he looking for something?*

She suddenly heard a disturbing sound in the vicinity of her living room, like the creak of a floorboard or rocking chair. Her muscles tensed up as she emerged quickly from the tub, dried herself, and put on her leopard-print bathrobe. The adrenaline in her veins was making her feel dizzy. Now she pushed open the bathroom door, ever so slightly, straining her ears for another sound. *Did I imagine it?*

* * * *

Over in the rectory, Maria was putting away the final dish from that night's supper. Although the priests' appetites were still lagging, at least they had both made an effort to praise the pecan pie she'd made for dessert. She had wanted to ask Father Bunt about the archbishop's visit, but she could tell by the look on his face that he probably didn't want much conversation, so she and Father William had done their best to talk about the weather.

Then Father Bunt had announced that he was going to drive over to Emory Hospital to visit patients, while Father William had headed for the Eternal Sunrise nursing home. She had fed Dopey a nice bowl of dog food and then tried to teach him the command to sit, but it was hopeless. She was beginning to wonder if the dog might be deaf, except he always understood the words "treat" and "walkie."

After she had taken Dopey out on a short jaunt, she left him in the kitchen with his rawhide bone and then locked up the rectory and headed home. Her heart was heavy with worry about Paul. But she knew her husband would be vindicated. She had been praying the Rosary for that intention every day, and the Blessed Mother had never let her down before.

* * * *

Making a quick Sign of the Cross, Francesca wrapped the robe more tightly around her and stepped into the hall. Then she peered into the living room. Much to her surprise, a matronly woman was sitting in the rocking chair with a younger woman—her daughter?—seated on the couch.

When she saw Francesca in the hall, the older woman jumped up from the chair. She had straw-like blonde hair, heavily bleached and teased into a style that used to be called a beehive, and she was wearing slacks that Francesca judged to be a size 3X. Across her generous bosom stretched a sweatshirt that announced "I Eat Moe's Pizza, Therefore I Am Happy." The woman, who looked to be in her sixties, wore a very apologetic expression as she stuck her hand out toward Francesca in a gesture of friendship. Francesca noticed there were tiny rhinestones glued to the tips of her pointy, painted nails.

"Honey, I sure hope we didn't give you a scare! I'm Cherie Cambio, Chip's mother—and this is my daughter, Chelsea. We wouldn'tve come in except the door was unlocked—and when I called out, there was no answer. We figgered we'd jes' set a spell till you showed up."

Francesca adjusted the sash on her robe while inwardly castigating herself for having left the door unlocked. *I couldn't hear them calling because the water was running.*

"Oh, no, you didn't scare me at all." She knew her face had to be giving her away. "Give me a moment to throw on some clothes, and I'll be right out. You make yourselves at home."

But just as the words left her lips, she realized their absurdity because clearly the two women had already done just that. She rushed into her bedroom and dressed quickly. Then she returned to the living room, trying to look nonplussed, as if it were an everyday occurrence to confront two uninvited strangers in her own home.

As she walked into the room, she saw Cherie Cambio gently rubbing Tubs's head and calling him a "big handsome guy," which seemed to please him, given the volume of purring.

Francesca's curiosity was getting the best of her. Maybe these women held the key to the murder investigation. She decided to act as if the visit were a perfectly normal occurrence.

"Would you like a soda or some coffee?"

"Anything diet is fine by me." Cherie tugged at the waistband of her slacks. "I'm trying to slim down a tad."

Chelsea, who appeared to be in her early thirties, was sporting a gold nose ring and six studs in her right ear lobe. She snapped her gum loudly before answering. Her words came out oddly muffled, but Francesca thought she said, "Whatever." She was wearing a shirt that proclaimed

"GRITS" across the front, and when she noticed Francesca's glance, she explained with a heavy lisp that it stood for "Girls Raised in the South."

Cherie looked pained. "Ever since she got that tongue ring, you cain't hardly understand a word that girl says. I don't understand young folks today." She directed her question at Francesca: "I mean, nose rings, sure. But why do y'all have to pierce y'all's tongues?"

Francesca figured this would not be the time to point out that there were millions of women in their thirties whose tongues were intact. Instead, she headed into the kitchen and returned with the sodas.

"Honey, you're probably wonderin' why we dropped in on you." Cherie took a long, loud swig of the diet drink. "Well, you know about my poor Chip . . ."

Here she broke down in tears and began groping around in a cavernous black canvas bag that had tiny, multicolored kangaroos parading across it. In seconds, she retrieved a wrinkled blue Kleenex.

"I'm so sorry about your son," Francesca said. "And your brother," she added, looking in Chelsea's direction.

"Whatever," Chelsea belched. "He was always getting into trouble."

Now the older woman tucked the blue Kleenex into her pocket, put her glass down on the coffee table with a resounding clink, and walked across the room. She was an imposing woman, hovering over the much thinner, shorter one seated on the couch.

"Young lady, don't you dare go bad-mouthin' your brother. My Chip was a good boy. He always took real good care of his momma."

Chelsea said nothing but just snapped her gum and concentrated on her drink.

Cherie now returned to the rocking chair, which let out an agonizing squeak as she settled her weight upon it. The chair was an antique that had been given to Dean by his grandmother, and Francesca envisioned it collapsing into a pile of sawdust before the night was through.

"You may not know this, honey, but Chip has a twin brother, Chuck," Cherie said. "Me and Chase—he's my husband—thought it would be real cute to name all the kids similar. And we sure wanted a mess of them." She smiled, revealing large yellow teeth. "I longed for a Cheryl or a Chad, but after the twins, we had Chelsea, and that was it."

"She named the dog Chi-Chi," Chelsea said. Francesca saw the mother hurl a stabbing look at Chelsea as she rearranged her weight in the protesting chair.

"We sent the boys to private high school, and even college —though Chelsea here didn't want none of it. But the boys got themselves a real good education. You probably remember how nice my Chip talked. People didn't even think him and Chuck were Southerners at all. Chip sounded real refined, didn't he, Chelsea?"

"Sure, Momma." The girl rolled her eyes.

"What brings you to Decatur?" Francesca was starting to worry that the twosome would be in her house all night, and she felt uneasy. Even if the door had been unlocked, it had been incredibly rude of two strangers to enter her house, and that was the bottom line.

"Well, honey, we're in town to pick up a few of Chip's things. We couldn't make it to the funeral because my husband came down with a bad spell of the flu. The doctors didn't think he would pull through, did they, Chelsea?"

Chelsea shrugged and Cherie continued. "But he come through it jes' fine, so here we are. Chip told us about the folks over at the church. He said you were a real fine lady, and I can see that's true."

Francesca didn't want to ask the obvious question: Why are you here tonight? She decided to wait until Chip's mother herself arrived at that point in her verbal journey. It took about another 30 minutes, during which time Francesca heard all about the trip from Mexico Beach, Florida, including each eatery they had frequented along the way. Cherie confessed to a liking for "Eye-talian" food and mentioned that her husband was of that nationality.

"Me, I'm part Cherokee and the rest Southerner, and my momma, may she rest in peace, wasn't too happy about me falling for a furriner. She didn't like Catholics none either. But I always say, 'To each his own.'"

Suddenly Cherie's face assumed an expression of great bliss, calling to Francesca's mind someone about to recount a mystical experience. In hushed tones, Cherie announced that the motel she and Chelsea were staying at had an all-you-can-eat waffle bar.

"Of course, I always skip lunch when I have waffles to start the day. I'm counting my carbo-hy-der-ates." She pronounced the final word in her sentence as if it were from a foreign language.

"First it was calories, then it was fat grams," Chelsea snorted. "I've told you a million times, Momma. You have to exercise." Chelsea looked at Francesca. "I jog every day, and I've told Momma she should come too."

"Can you jes' imagine me joggin'?" Cherie countered, looking at Francesca.

Francesca had a momentary mental image of an elephant with a blonde beehive in a running suit and Nikes. She decided it had to be a rhetorical question.

"That jes' ain't my style," Cherie continued. "When it comes to exercise, I like to shake my booty with my husband. We got us some real nice country music places back home."

The glasses were now empty, and Francesca was getting antsy. She was about to glance meaningfully at the grandfather clock, but before she could, Cherie did something that took Francesca's breath away. The big woman suddenly plunged her hand into the depths of her purse and, after a few seconds, extracted a small gun. She then pointed it directly at Francesca.

Cherie's hand was shaking. "Honey, I got a favor to ask you, and if you jes' follow along, then everything will go smooth and no one will get hurt."

CHAPTER 12

Gun in hand, Cherie edged her bulk slowly from the chair. "You see, we need some of Chip's things that are at the church, and we know you have a key. So, don't worry none, honey. We jes' want you to take us over there so we can get his things."

Chelsea cackled and slapped her knee as if her mother had told an uproarious joke. "Yeah, things like money. That's what Momma's after."

"You hush your mouth, girl, you understand?" Cherie snapped. "I don't want no more back talk from you." She waved the gun at Francesca. "Now, come on. Go get your keys. We're going to take us a little ride over to church."

Francesca looked nervously at the gun. She couldn't believe this was happening. It felt like one of those bad dreams where you can't wake up. It was possible the gun wasn't loaded because Cherie kept pointing it wildly in various directions, even at her own daughter. Still, Francesca wasn't taking any chances, so she obediently stood up, got her keys, and went with the women to their parked car outside. Chelsea drove, while Cherie and Francesca sat in the back. The floor was littered with empty potato chip bags, plus old wrappings from fast-food restaurants. There was a stale aroma of French fries.

Cherie kept up a steady stream of chatter during the short ride over to the church, and she kept apologizing for the gun. "I don't usually do things this way, honey, but I didn't see no other way this time. So you sit tight and everything will be fine."

When they arrived at Saint Rita's rectory, Francesca noticed glumly there were no cars parked outside, which meant the priests and Maria were gone. She wondered what Cherie would have done if other people had been there. Would she have stormed in anyway, poking the gun in Francesca's back, using her as a hostage to scare everyone into compliance?

Hands trembling, Francesca unlocked the door to the rectory, wishing she had not been given a master key. The two women bustled in. Dopey was sound asleep by the kitchen door and didn't even blink an eye when the threesome entered. *Some watchdog.*

Francesca unlocked Chip's office door for them, and Cherie handed the gun to her daughter and went inside. Francesca could hear her rummaging through drawers and cursing. Somehow the thought of Chelsea with the gun was even more unnerving than Cherie, and Francesca felt dizzy and nauseated from fear. *Are these women capable of murder?*

She had been praying that one of the priests would come home, but then she feared that they might be injured, so she simply prayed for her own safety. *Sweet Jesus, watch over me. Holy Saint Joseph, pray for me.*

Suddenly Cherie came tearing out of the office. Without a word she grabbed the gun from Chelsea. "OK, I got what we need. You tie her up so we can get a good head start, and then we'll get out of here."

Chelsea pouted. "Tie her up? I don't want to! I don't know how."

"For Heaven's sake, quit whining! Do I have to do everything?"

In the end, it was Cherie who pulled a roll of strapping tape from her purse and clumsily bound Francesca's hands behind her back and then wrapped her ankles together, immobilizing her. As she did so, she kept apologizing. "This ain't the way I was brought up, and my momma, rest her soul, would hate to see me now."

After the twosome hurried off into the night, Francesca lay quietly in the corner of Chip's office where they had left her. *At least I'm still alive. And I know someone will come home soon.*

Just then, the door inched open, and Dopey ambled in. He approached her in a humble way with his head bowed low and his tail wagging furiously and then gently licked her face. Then, perhaps puzzled by her immobility, he sat up and extended his paw. Then he fetched a ball and brought it to her, and rolled over a few times. Finally, much to her delight, he decided to howl, good and loud.

* * * *

Tony drove by Francesca's house and noticed her car parked outside and the lights on, so he decided to stop by. It was high time he apologized and got the whole thing between them ironed out. But when he found the front door unlocked, he got a bad feeling and went inside. He could tell she had been entertaining two other people, and by the lipstick marks on the glasses, they had to be women.

He did a quick check of her house, noting the bathtub full of still-warm water and her bathrobe thrown on the floor in her bedroom. She had left in a hurry with her visitors, but why? And why was the door left unlocked? He was going to call her on her cell phone, but then he saw it lying on the dining room table. She usually took it with her whenever she went out, so something was definitely wrong.

Some instinct told him to drive by the rectory. He noticed there were no cars outside, and no lights on, but he definitely heard a noise and realized it was a dog howling. *Something's not right here.* He grabbed his flashlight, got out of his car, and discovered that the front door was ajar. He rushed inside and followed the sound of the howling down the hall, where he found Francesca. She was crying, but she was uninjured. *Thank God!*

* * * *

Once he had removed the tape from her ankles and wrists and helped her to her feet, Francesca's tears flowed heavily. "I was more scared than I thought. I don't think that gun was loaded, but it could have been, and they might have . . ."

Here she broke down again, and he took her hand reassuringly. "You're safe now. Now start from the beginning."

She told him about the two women and gave him a description of the car, although she had not seen the license plate number. He called in the information to the station and added that the twosome was probably headed back to Mexico Beach.

"Did they tell you where they were staying?"

She rubbed her wrists. "All I know is it has an all-you-can-eat waffle bar."

She watched as Tony did a quick check of Chip's office, which had been left in a shambles. He explained to her that if Chip had been stealing items from the church, it was likely that the mother and sister knew about this, and they probably were trying to figure out where he had hid them. They also might have been looking for a key to a safety-deposit box, and since they had left so quickly, they had probably found it.

"But did they really expect to find written directions about where he hid the stuff?"

"Well, it's hard to say. From your description, they don't sound like masters of logic. They might just have been chasing a hunch. And if they really did find the key, then it paid off."

"But didn't someone already search his office?"

Tony nodded. "We didn't find a key—but we didn't pull up the carpet like they did."

"What do we do now?" Francesca was exhausted, but she still had enough energy to give Dopey a lavish round of petting. *If he were a cat, he'd be purring.*

"I think we should get you home. You've had a terrible shock tonight. I'll leave a note for the priests, so they'll know what happened, and tell them not to disturb Chip's office any further until it's been dusted for prints."

Francesca heard the sound of the front door opening. Father Bunt evidently had noticed the police car outside because she heard him calling out, "Is anyone here? Is anything wrong?"

After filling in Father Bunt on the latest development, Tony gently escorted Francesca to his truck and drove her home. She was feeling extremely sleepy, probably from the stress, but she also admitted she was hungry.

"Well, you know the two things I can cook are waffles and grilled-cheese sandwiches. Which would you like?"

"I think I'll stay away from waffles for a while. But a cheese sandwich would be divine."

When they entered her living room, she automatically reached for the glasses to clean up, but he stopped her. "Just leave them there, since I want them dusted for prints. We'll want to double check the women's identities and figure out if they have a record."

"Oh, that's OK; it gives me an excuse to be lazy." She settled down on the couch, and Tubs meowed to be picked up and placed on her lap. He was getting too old to leap up as he had in his youth. She heard Tony in the kitchen, making comforting sounds that reminded her of Dean: little crashes now and again, an occasional "whoops," a few "oh, nos!" and then out he came, carrying a slightly charred grilled-cheese sandwich and a glass of white wine. Neither of them said a word about their argument the other night.

"Look, Francesca, I can't stay long. I have to follow up on this at the station. But I wanted you to know about that woman . . . Mrs. Feeny . . . I'll be seeing her tomorrow. She may be able to clear Paul's name."

"That would be wonderful."

"Yeah, but if so, we'll be back to square one. The killer may still be out there, so be careful."

This was her chance, she realized. *I should apologize, but I'm too tired. Besides, he's just doing all this as part of his job. I can tell by his expression.*

The next morning, Francesca slept later than usual. As she climbed out of bed, she noticed that her wrists and ankles were sore and developing bruises. She yawned and helped Tubs down off the bed. By the time she had fallen asleep, it had been well after midnight, but she had slept soundly, knowing that Tony was outside keeping watch.

"There's always a chance they might come back because they forgot something, and I'm not leaving you unprotected for the night," he had explained.

After she had showered and dressed, she peeked outside and saw his truck was still there. She waved to let him know she was awake and then invited him in for coffee. There was still an odd tension between them. They talked about what had happened the night before, but neither one broached what Francesca was privately thinking of as "the incident."

"Could I make you some breakfast?" she asked as she handed him a mug of coffee. *Please stay longer, and please stop being so officious.*

But he shook his head. "Just coffee, thanks. I'm going home to get some sleep, but there will be other officers swinging by during the day to be sure you're OK. If you go out, be sure to keep your cell phone with you—and for Heaven's sake, Francesca, lock the door!"

As he left, she felt alone and sad. *That's it. The romance really is over.*

Francesca had no unusual visitors that day, and in the afternoon, Tony called to tell her the status of the case.

"We're trying to find out where Chip's safety-deposit box might be located. There aren't that many banks in Mexico Beach, but he might have chosen a larger town nearby. We've checked his family home there, but his father didn't seem to know much. He said the wife and daughter were away visiting family. The old guy's just out of the hospital, and it's possible he doesn't have a clue what's going on."

Then, after a few niceties, there was an awkward pause. She waited for him to bring up the topic that had wedged its way between them. But all he said was, "Oh, I've got another call to take. I've gotta go." And that was it.

The next day, Francesca returned morosely to her phone duties at the rectory. She looked glumly at the little calendar in her purse, which was painfully empty of notes indicating future dinner dates with Tony. The calls were light, and she was using the free time to update the Mass schedule in the big calendar book at the desk. Parishioners would offer donations to have Masses celebrated for deceased family members and friends, as well as for the special intentions of the living. The little cross by a name indicated that the person was dead; otherwise, there were the letters "SI" for a person's special intentions.

As she was looking for an open date to have a Mass celebrated for Dean, she noticed something extremely odd.

Someone had given a donation to have a Mass said for the repose of the soul of Chip Cambio on a Sunday after Thanksgiving. That in itself was certainly not unusual, but she felt her stomach turn over when she noticed when the request had been made—two weeks before his death.

She did some research in the files and soon discovered who had requested the Mass. She sat there for a few minutes, feeling stunned. It couldn't be true, but she had the evidence right in front of her eyes. Sister Therese! *Is it possible that she's the murderer?*

She sat staring at the phone, thinking. How would Sister have known that Chip would be in the library that particular night, working on the books? Then she remembered what Tony had told her: Chip had let slip to Sister Therese his real plan to get rid of the old hymnals. Perhaps he had also told her when he would be in the library implementing his plan. As for the Mass, Sister probably didn't think anyone would check to see when it had been requested—or by whom. But why on Earth request a Mass for someone you planned to kill? *Guilty conscience?*

The phones were quiet. Francesca sat at the desk, straightening up the drawers as she reflected on what she'd just discovered. The process of tossing out old sticky notes and lining up pencils relaxed her, helping her sort through her thoughts. The Mass book was incriminating; there was no doubt in her mind, but there was something else bothering her that she couldn't quite bring to consciousness.

She walked over to the window, noting that the African violet plant on the sill was starting to droop. She went down the hall and filled up a glass from the water dispenser, and then poured it in the planter. Some of the water spilled onto the floor, and she grabbed some paper towels and began mopping it up. As she was doing these mindless tasks, she heard the sounds of children laughing outside, and she suddenly had an image of the school playground.

She remembered the day when she had seen Chip arguing with a nun on the playground. Chip was about six feet tall, and Francesca recalled that the woman looked just a few inches shorter. On a hunch, she opened a desk drawer and pulled out the church directory. There, in the front of the book was a photo of the seven Dominican sisters who taught at Saint Rita's school. They were standing in front of a statue of the Blessed Mother, smiling into the sun. Her heart beat a little faster as she noticed that six of the sisters were quite short, but one towered over all of them. It was Sister Therese.

So she's the sister I saw that day having that big argument with Chip. She imagined Tony nodding at her and saying, "Now you're starting to build a real case. Good work."

Chapter 13

Later that day, Francesca went back to Saint Rita's to pray in the little chapel. She needed quiet time to figure out what to do next. There was no one else there, so she assumed that the person who had signed up to be a guardian of the Eucharist had had a last-minute emergency. *It's you and me, Jesus, all alone.*

At the thought "alone," she felt her eyes burning with tears. She missed Tony terribly, but she wasn't about to go running after him. If he really cared about her, she knew he would apologize for their disagreement the other night, and she would then be willing to admit she'd been to blame as well. But they had reached a classic stalemate. She pulled out her rosary beads. *Maybe the Blessed Mother will help me.*

She had just completed her prayers when she heard the door to the chapel open. She was aware that the person had taken a seat in the pew behind her, but tried to refrain from turning around to see who it was. After a few moments, though, her curiosity got the best of her. She was very startled to be looking into the face of none other than Chuck Cambio.

He had shaved off his beard and was wearing sunglasses, no doubt in an effort to hide his identity from parishioners, but it was definitely Chuck.

He spoke in a whisper: "I saw your car outside. Could you join me for a cup of coffee once you're through?"

She nodded. "I'll just be a few minutes." She heard him go out the back door, and then she thought about what she was doing. *But what harm is there in a cup of coffee? It's not like there's a long line of men clamoring to spend time with me.* And she had to admit: a traditional Catholic with Chip's good looks was an attractive combination.

He was waiting outside, hunched over the literature table as if he were reading something. Now she was suddenly nervous about going with him. *The rest of the family is so weird. What if he's as strange as his mother and sister?*

He must have read the expression of doubt on her face. "Look, I realize you don't know me very well." He picked up a little pamphlet about Saint Augustine. "But I really hope you'll hear me out. I'm very concerned about what's happening to Chip."

"What do you mean, happening to him?"

"Can't you see? He was the victim, the one found murdered, but the police are more interested in turning him into a criminal than they are in solving the case. It's all over the papers about the missing items from the church, and even though there's no proof, everyone is jumping to conclusions." He crumpled the little pamphlet. "It just steams me that all this is happening. Look, Chip was no Saint, but a thief? I just don't think so. Wouldn't it make more sense that the murderer stole the stuff?"

She nodded. She hated to admit it, but it did seem like Chip had been turned into a criminal, and he had no way to defend himself. The surprise appearance of his mother and sister at her house, however, certainly suggested he had been up to no good. Maybe Chuck could shed some light on that.

"I guess I see your point. Well, where do you want to go for coffee?"

He removed his sunglasses now and she could see the relief in his eyes. "Let's go somewhere where there's no chance we'll run into parishioners. I'm still trying to remain incognito."

* * * *

Father William was in his room, praying. He was extremely relieved to see order slowly returning to the parish. The red *Worship II* hymnals were back in the pews, and a new choir director had been hired, one who was well versed in the traditional music of the Church. Although many people at Saint Rita's were still troubled by the terrible event that had happened, they also seemed relieved that the perpetrator had been apprehended. *I hope they have the right man. But even if they do, Father Bunt's not going to rest easy until the money is found.*

Maria was a wreck, which was entirely understandable. She continued to cook and do other chores, but he could tell by her face that her heart was no longer in it. She rarely talked about the case, but her eyes seemed permanently red from crying. His heart went out to her. He couldn't imagine what it would be like to have someone you loved and trusted being a suspect in a murder case.

At least she doesn't have to worry about Ignatius being on the loose any more. The hamster trap had finally worked. It was a pleasure to once again hear the little fellow chirping contentedly now and again.

"Ignatius is in his cage, God's in His Heaven, and all's right with the world," Father William murmured, tailoring one of his mother's favorite sayings.

He looked out his window and spotted Francesca walking with a man. There was something very familiar about him. Father William put on his stronger glasses to take another look, and recoiled in shock. *Cambio! Impossible!*

* * * *

Francesca and Chuck ended up at a cafe in midtown Atlanta, about three miles from Saint Rita's. She noted that the restaurant hosted the usual eclectic Atlanta crowd: a few teenage girls with Mohawk hairdos, accompanied by guys with tattoos running from stem to stern; a sweaty father in running attire who had evidently been out jogging with a toddler, who sat dozing in a stroller; a few people sitting alone, tapping away on laptops; and an overweight sixtyish woman in a purple running suit, yakking loudly into her Bluetooth headset about an upcoming hemorrhoid operation.

As soon as they had their coffee, Chuck apologized profusely. "Look, I got wind of what my mother and sister did the other night, and I can't tell you how sorry I am. I can't believe they're running around with guns and doing all these crazy things."

He paused to take a sip of coffee and then added sugar. "I should tell you, however, that the gun was definitely not loaded. My dad tried to teach them a long time ago how to use a gun and declared it hopeless. But he told my mother to keep an unloaded gun with her at all times because most folks are not going to argue when they see a gun. He wanted her to have it for protection, not for . . ." Here his voice seemed to dwindle.

Francesca added a packet of sugar to her coffee, even though she usually took it just with cream. It would give her more time to think. How did he know about the women's visit to her house? It was probably in the newspaper, although she couldn't be sure. She had missed reading it the past few days. What if he were in cahoots with his mother and sister? She shuddered slightly. *Maybe he has a gun—and it's really loaded.*

He peered at her across the table. "Are you OK? I noticed that you just shivered."

"Oh, it's just the air-conditioning."

Chuck looked around nervously as if afraid someone from the church might spot him. *He's acting like someone who's guilty. But what is he guilty of? Oh, I should have told Tony about him.* At the thought of Tony, though, her spirits sank. *As far as he's concerned, the case is closed. Over and done with—just like our relationship.*

"Chuck, you seem so sure your brother had nothing to do with the thefts. But why in the world did your mother and sister take me hostage then and go rummaging through his office? It sure looks like they were searching for the stuff he'd stolen—and the money."

He licked his lips. "Yeah, I know it looks bad. But believe me, there's an explanation. You see, Chip used to send my mom and Chelsea money pretty regularly."

Now he sighed. "Let me start at the beginning. When you look up 'dysfunctional' in the dictionary, you'll see a picture of my family. My mom goes through money like it's water, and Chelsea's just a lazy mooch. My dad drinks, so he can't be relied on."

"It sounds pretty bad."

"Yeah, childhood was . . . anything but idyllic, I assure you. But Chip and I somehow avoided the worst of it. Back before my dad's drinking got out of control, my parents scraped up enough money to send us to private high school and then college. Thanks to them, we managed to escape the world we came from." Now he tugged nervously at his chin, as if momentarily forgetting the beard was gone.

"Long story short, Chip saw himself as the grateful, dutiful son, sending them money like that—although I think he was just enabling them. In any event, when he died, the gravy train ran dry. Then my mom panicked—and you saw the end result of that."

He looked down at the table. "She and Chelsea were looking for money, or a bank book or something, and I guess they found it."

Now he reached across the table and took her hand. "And I'm *really* sorry about what happened to you."

"It wasn't your fault, Chuck. And I . . . I . . . really didn't realize the family situation. I guess I just jumped to conclusions."

She felt herself drawn to him suddenly. It was rare for a man to open up to her like he had. Her doubts about him dissolved as he gently kept her hand in his.

"Look, Francesca, I've been doing some investigating on my own. Somehow I doubt the police have the right guy in jail. They tend to jump to conclusions too quickly. My guess is they'll eventually let the guy go and forget all about finding the real murderer."

She needed time to think. She added more sugar to her coffee. When she sipped it, she realized it was now sickeningly sweet.

"You know lots of people in the parish," he said. "They're the most likely suspects, right? I mean, they're the ones he might have irritated, right? So, tell me, who do you think did it?"

She wasn't sure if she was doing the right thing, but she was eager to share her hunch with someone. When she told him the name, he looked surprised.

"A sister? Are you sure?"

"Well, she's only been in the convent about five years, and she's got quite a temper. I mean, she's not your typical *Sound of Music* nun."

After she explained about the Mass book, he looked thoughtful. "That does sound strange, I have to admit, but is that the only evidence?"

It was then she told him about the scene she'd witnessed on the playground. "They were really shouting at each other. She looked like she wanted to hit him."

He nodded. "We could be on to something here."

* * * *

Father Bunt rubbed his eyes as he looked over the stack of mail on his desk. The money missing from the building fund still hadn't been found and neither had the chalices and other valuable items. Father Bunt had been putting on a cheery face for the past few days because he felt he owed it to poor William, who was new to the priesthood and deserved better than him for a boss. But the strain was wearing on him. Every time the phone rang, he jumped. Every time he looked through the mail, he cringed in fear. He was terrified that any day now the archbishop would transfer him to some parish in the South Georgia swamps.

There was a sharp knock at his door, and he saw Father William standing in the threshold, looking quite pale and shaken.

"What is it, man? Have you seen a ghost or something?"

"That's just it, Father. I think I have indeed seen a ghost."

* * * *

Francesca hoped the plan would work. Chuck had assured her that if they confronted Sister Therese, she would say something incriminating. Francesca had to admit that his words made sense. If she had ever done something as terrible as committing murder, she could not imagine confronting someone who looked identical to the victim. Wouldn't she break down and make a full confession? That was what Chuck was banking on. He drove her back to the church to get her car, and then they agreed to meet the next day to implement the plan.

Her role, he said, would be simple enough: She would go to visit Sister on some pretext, and she and Sister would be sitting there, chatting, when Chuck would knock on the door and come in. She and Chuck would be witnesses to whatever happened next, and he would also have a hidden tape recorder.

The whole scenario sounded fairly straightforward, and she was eager for it to be over so she could alert Tony. She hated keeping the plan from him, but Chuck had insisted that if the police were in on it, everything could easily backfire.

"The police are all about rules and regulations," he'd said. "They'd send over a cop car, go over her rights, then Sister would clam up and deny everything—and tell us to talk to her lawyer." Here he had run his fingers through his hair impatiently. "Once that happened, all bets would be off."

Then he had smiled at her in a particularly endearing way. "You have to trust my instincts on this. Believe me, everything will go fine. And as soon as we have the evidence on the tape recorder, we'll go directly to the police, I promise."

Then he had suddenly changed the subject. "Francesca, I don't mean to get personal here, but are you dating anyone? You know, seriously?"

"Well, I do have a boyfriend, but right now we're sort of . . . well . . . on the outs."

"Well then, why don't you and I get together, say, next Friday for a movie and dinner?"

He had given her such an earnest look that she had agreed.

Once she was home, though, Francesca started having a serious case of nerves. *What if Chuck's real plan is to get revenge on the person who killed his brother*? Chuck seemed to have little faith in the police getting things right, so he might want to take matters into his own hands. *What if his plan is to be judge, jury, and executioner?*

There was something about his distrust of the police and their "rules and regulations" that set off a little warning bell in her head. Rules and regulations were what kept people safe. *Has he had some bad experiences with the police he doesn't want to mention?*

As she was mulling over the situation, the phone rang. It was Margaret Hennessy.

"Francesca, I just remembered: I still have Chip's letters. Shall I put them in your desk—and then you could give them to Tony? I hate holding onto them."

"I'll be right over."

An hour later, Francesca was back at home with the letters in her hands. She sat down on the couch and began poring over them. Although much of it was junk mail, one letter stood out. It was from Chip's mother.

> *Thanks for the last check. Your such a good boy. Chelsea aint feeling so good we have doctor bills to pay. Let me know when you and Chuck get the money from the church. He said you were going 50-50—but dont forget your momma.*

There was more, but that was all Francesca needed to read. Her hands had turned icy with fear. *It's time I told Tony all about this. I can't let our lovers' quarrel get in the way. It's just too dangerous.* She dialed the station, but got his voice mail. She didn't want to leave a complicated message, so she simply said, "Tony, I have information on the case. Please call me." She also tried his cell phone, but he had turned it off. *He must be in a meeting.*

After a half hour had passed, she found herself getting antsy. Finally she resolved to go see Sister Therese herself, immediately. *If she's the murderer, I should be able to figure it out—and then I'll leave and call the police. If she's not . . . I'll warn her about Chuck.*

* * * *

Sister Therese was in her room in the small convent adjacent to Saint Rita's rectory, where she and six other sisters lived. All of them taught at Saint Rita's school and also oversaw numerous ministries at the church. She was putting the final touches on a yellow-and-white baby blanket that she was knitting for her youngest sister, Pam, who was due in about a month. She had her supplies neatly arranged on the table next to her, the skeins of pale-colored wool along with scissors and a tape measure.

Now Sister Therese jumped slightly as the train shuddered below the ground, jolting her hands just enough to cause her to drop a stitch. *Blast! I'll never get used to that subway. I wish the city had realized that a church should be a place of peace and quiet.* At that thought, she winced. It certainly had not been a peaceful place when Chip Cambio had taken over. She had heard an old saying that the devil is most busy at the foot of the altar. And given what she had seen with Chip's performance, she had to agree. She could feel her blood pressure rising just thinking about some of the stunts he had pulled. Now she put down the knitting and stood up. *That's all over now.*

* * * *

"William, you know as well as I do that there is no such thing as a ghost!" Father Bunt thundered.

The younger man felt sheepish as he took a seat opposite the pastor's. He was beginning to doubt his own eyes. He was starting to think that what he had seen was a man who strongly resembled Chip. *He didn't even have a beard.* He had been so sure a few moments ago that he would have wagered anything on the fact that it had been Chip himself. Now he was embarrassed because he knew his claim sounded preposterous.

"Well, Father, I guess my eyes were deceiving me." Father William took off his glasses and rubbed his eyes. "It must have been someone who resembled Chip very strongly."

Father Bunt looked concerned. "Look, William, I know things have been strange—that's an understatement—at the parish lately. I haven't been there for you like I wanted to be." Now a tear seemed to glisten in his eyes. "I've really failed you."

The younger priest was horrified. There was nothing he wanted less than to upset the pastor, who already was so burdened.

"Oh, please, Father, don't say that. You've been perfectly fine. It's not your fault at all."

"Every damn thing that has gone wrong here is my fault, William, and I'm starting to realize that now. It's not just Chip's death and the missing money either. I've failed you and Maria and the whole crew here at Saint Rita's."

Now he stood up and walked over to the younger man. He reached out his hand. "But I'm going to make it up to you. You just have to promise me one thing."

Father William clasped the outstretched hand and nodded, waiting for whatever came next.

"You must come to me whenever you are troubled, whenever you need to talk. I won't ever be too busy to see you. Do you understand?"

Father William was now thoroughly embarrassed. He knew how much pressure the pastor was under, and he was just adding to the burden. He was kicking himself mentally for ever having knocked on the door.

"Of course, Father. Please don't trouble yourself any more about . . . about . . . what I saw . . . or, rather, what I thought I saw."

"No trouble at all. I'm here whenever you need me! And William?"

"Yes, Father?"

"Take a break for the rest of the day. You're working yourself too hard."

Chapter 14

Sister Therese's phone rang. It was the sister at the reception area of the convent, announcing a visitor. When Sister Therese heard Francesca's name, she immediately said, "Send her right through."

A few moments later, Sister opened the door with a big smile.

"Francesca! What a nice surprise. What brings you here?"

The woman came in, but she seemed so nervous.

"I just wanted to talk with you a little while, Sister."

"Certainly, come on in and sit down and I'll make you a nice cup of tea."

"I . . . can only stay a minute." Francesca perched on the edge of the chair as if she thought it would collapse into pieces at any moment.

Maybe she's having some kind of romantic trouble and is looking for advice, thought Therese.

"Francesca, is there something troubling you?"

Francesca picked up a small piece of yarn and wrapped it around her fingers. "I think it's just Chip's death, Sister. I have this . . . well . . . this odd jumble of emotions."

Sister nodded, waiting for more.

"I . . . well, of course I'm sorry he's dead, but at the same time, Sister, he was such a . . . such a . . ." Her hands circled the air as if trying to grasp the right word.

"Pain in the rear end?"

Francesca smiled weakly. "Yes, that's the thing, Sister. He seemed to delight in making changes that went against so much of what I believe in. So much of what is really Church teaching, if you know what I mean."

Sister patted Francesca's hand. "Of course I do. But every parish has people like him—maybe not so . . . well . . . in your face as he was—but as annoying as they might be, our job isn't to change them. We just have to continue living out our faith and setting a good example."

Sister inwardly blanched at her own words. *That sounds like Mary Poppins.*

"Yes, Sister, I realize that. But you don't think that maybe his death was somehow . . ." Francesca's voice trailed off.

"Somehow what, dear?"

Francesca was tying little knots in the piece of yarn. "Well, maybe there was someone in the parish, who thought killing Chip was justified because of all the harm he was causing. What do you think . . ." She abruptly changed her tone. "Who do you think killed him?"

Sister sat up straighter in her chair and looked out the window. "Well, certainly not Paul. That's a real stretch on the police's part, in my opinion."

Francesca nodded eagerly. "That's exactly how I feel. I think the murderer is still out there somewhere."

"Yes, it does seem that he—or *she*—certainly is. This means you should be very careful, Francesca, you do realize that?" Sister's expression was grave.

Francesca shivered. "Yes, I do, Sister." Now she forced a little laugh. "Tony keeps reminding me to lock my door."

Sister started organizing the skeins of wool. "Tony? Oh, yes, that's right—you've been dating that policeman, haven't you?"

"Yes, although we haven't seen each other for a while now."

Francesca took a deep, audible breath, as if gathering up her courage. "Sister, there's something I need to tell you."

"What's that, dear?" Sister Therese picked up the scissors that she kept near her wool.

The phone rang and Francesca stood up suddenly, as if startled. Sister murmured, "Excuse me," and answered it.

"Father Bunt? Well, certainly, send him right in."

* * * *

The knock came at the door seconds later, and Sister answered it.

"Father Bunt! I'm just talking with Francesca. Please come in."

"What's with the scissors, Sister?"

"Oh, these!" She smiled. "I've been working on some knitting."

Father Bunt was surprised to see Francesca in Sister's room. Judging from the troubled look on her face, he surmised Francesca was there to get some kind of counseling. *I hope she doesn't think she's seen a ghost.*

"Sister, I won't keep you long," he said. "I just wanted you to know the good news: Maria's husband has been cleared of the crime and is back home with his family."

Sister Therese looked Heavenward. "Oh, thanks be to God!"

"Yes, it's great news, Father," Francesca said. "But that still leaves the big question, right?"

He nodded. "Yes, we still don't know who the perpetrator is."

"I was just mentioning to Francesca," Sister said, "that we all have to be really careful if there's a killer on the loose, don't we?"

"That's for sure," Father Bunt said. "Well, I can't stay long, Sister. I know you've been praying for Paul, and I wanted to give you the good news in person."

The phone rang again, and Sister answered it with a look of mock exasperation. "Yes? Who? Oh, my . . . no, don't worry: that must be his brother. Send him over."

* * * *

Tony saw the light blinking on his phone but decided to check his messages later. He had a big stack of paper on his desk that he had to get through first. He had done a thorough background check on Chip Cambio and discovered some very interesting things. For one, the man had a police record. In his twenties, he had put in some prison time in Florida for breaking and entering and had been picked up a number of times for various misdemeanors.

Some of what Chip had told Father Bunt checked out as true. After college he had enrolled in a seminary, but he had left after a year. It was also true that he had worked as a liturgist in some churches in north Florida. And, just as Bunt had discovered, these churches had reported small sums of money missing during the time Chip had worked there. But there never seemed to be enough evidence to pin anything definite on him. *And this was the man who was calling the shots at Saint Rita's.*

The mother and sister had been apprehended in Mexico Beach when they had attempted to open a safety-deposit box registered to Chip. Tony had managed to trace the bank account where Chip had transferred the church funds. He had also found a receipt in Chip's office showing that Chip had invested the money in gold coins. Tony had contacted the bank in Florida about the situation. When he found out that Chip had a box there, he had asked to be alerted the moment anyone tried to get into it. According to the bank's records, Chip had shown up in person at the bank—a few days before his death—to rent the box. He then had evidently driven back to Decatur and hidden the key in his office. *But why hide it?* Tony got up from his desk and went to the vending machine down the hall, where he bought a bag of corn chips and pondered the question. *Maybe Chip was worried that someone might come looking for the key. Someone who knew about the gold perhaps. But who?*

Cherie and Chelsea had been taken into custody, although at first they both disavowed ever having been in Decatur. But when asked about holding Francesca at gunpoint, the mother had inadvertently admitted their guilt by assuring the police officer, "Honey, it wasn't even loaded!" The daughter had broken down when arrested and given the police plenty of vital information about Chip. She explained that his usual way of operating had been to steal just enough cash to survive without making the thefts too obvious. But then when he was hired at Saint Rita's, something had changed. He had learned about the large sum of cash in the building fund, and when he was given his own account at the church, the temptation had evidently proven too great for him. He had told Chelsea that he was planning one final, very large heist, after which he was going to get out of the liturgist business, once and for all.

Now the money would be returned to the church, but there were still some valuable items missing—worth many thousands of dollars and sacred to boot. The Cambio family residence in Florida had been thoroughly searched, but none of the items had turned up. What had happened to them was anyone's guess at this point. Neither Cherie nor Chelsea had any idea; or if they did, they weren't talking.

Tony threw the empty chip bag into the trash can near his desk. Now that Paul was out of jail, there was no real suspect in the murder case. The mother and sister had been out that night dancing at a country-western bar, where the bartender, bouncer, and others were willing to vouch for their presence. Tony hated that the murderer was out there on the loose, maybe planning to strike again.

There was something Chip's father had told him that kept niggling at him. Evidently Chip had an identical twin brother. Was it possible the two were working in tandem, pilfering money from various churches? Maybe Chip had tried to double-cross his brother—at the cost of his life. Or maybe the brother wanted this last big score all to himself. But where was he now? The father claimed he hadn't seen Chuck Cambio in months. The mother and the sister had said the same thing.

Speaking of months, I've gotta do something about Francesca. This is ridiculous, going so long without getting together. I acted like an ass that night, and it's time to tell her. He thought about calling her cell phone, but she had a habit of turning it off. *A bad habit, just like leaving the door unlocked.* He tried her number at home. When he got her answering machine, he left a quick message: "It's Tony. Look, I want to see you—and soon. We need to talk."

* * * *

Sister Therese opened the door. "Oh, you gave Sister Mary Louise quite a start! Do come in, and I'll introduce you to the others."

What the heck is Chuck doing here? Francesca thought nervously. *He said the plan was to visit Sister tomorrow.* He shot her a dark look that seemed to be asking the same thing about her.

Father Bunt jumped out of his chair and was staring at Chuck as if he were seeing an apparition. "So that explains it."

"Explains what?" Sister asked, as she put the scissors away in the table drawer.

"Oh, nothing, really. It's just that I didn't realize . . ." His voice trailed off.

"I'm forgetting my manners," Sister said. "I'm Sister Therese, of course. Father Bunt, Francesca Bibbo, this is Chip's brother, Chuck Cambio.

Chuck nodded at Sister and extended a hand to Father Bunt. And then he turned slowly to face Francesca.

"Pleased to meet you," he muttered.

Francesca avoided his eyes. "Good to meet you, too," she said in a very small voice.

Chuck now turned his attention to Sister Therese. "I didn't realize you knew my brother so well. I didn't think the people at church knew Chip had a twin."

"Please, have a seat." Sister waved her hand at a chair adjacent to Father Bunt's. "Oh, Chip told me plenty of things. We weren't exactly the best of friends, and we certainly had our differences, but one night he mentioned what it had been like growing up with a . . . I think he said a double."

"So you and Chip were . . . *friends?*" Father Bunt interjected.

Sister nodded. "Well, at first, to be honest, he rubbed me the wrong way, to put it mildly. But after a while, I realized he'd been sent as a kind of challenge from the Lord. I mean, how could the man change, how could he come around to the right way of doing things, if everyone rejected him?" She picked up a skein of wool and squeezed it lightly.

"So, yes, we were friends."

Chuck let out a bitter little laugh. "Friends, huh?" He shot Francesca another look. "That's very interesting."

Francesca noticed that Chuck's brow was furrowed. He seemed very agitated. *Maybe it's because I surprised him by being here. Maybe he's figured out that I was going to tell Sister the plan—or maybe he's afraid I've already told her.*

"Did I interrupt a prayer meeting here or something?" Chuck looked at Sister.

"No, nothing like that." Sister smiled. "Actually, we were talking about your brother . . . Oh, I apologize: I must tell you how very sorry I am about his death."

Chuck winced. "Thanks."

"Yes, it's a terrible thing," Father Bunt added. "A real tragedy." Then he glanced at his watch. "Well, it's good to have met you, Chuck, but I'm afraid I have a meeting, so . . ."

But he never finished the sentence because at that moment, Chuck thrust his hand into his pocket and withdrew a pistol. Sister inhaled sharply, making an odd hissing sound, and Father Bunt said, "Good Lord, man, what are you doing?"

Trembling, Francesca shrank back in her chair, wrapping her arms tightly across her chest. *He's going to kill us all. What a fool I was to ever trust him.*

"Just be quiet and do what you're told, and no one gets hurt," Chuck snapped, standing up.

As he did, Francesca slowly inched her hand into her pocket, felt for her cell phone, and pressed the number one on the keypad—the speed dial for Tony. Almost simultaneously, Father Bunt rose from his chair.

"Look, this is no way to behave. We've had enough trouble already."

But Chuck edged closer to Father Bunt and pointed the gun directly at his head. "Back off, Father, if you know what's good for you."

Father Bunt sat down.

"And you!" Chuck turned to Francesca. "Hands out of your pockets. You think I'm blind?"

* * * *

Tony had information on the twin brother's car and license plate number and ran a quick check. He was startled to realize that the man had received a speeding ticket just yesterday—and the record showed he had been driving in Decatur. *This guy could be the murderer, but even if he's not, he still might have some of the loot from the church stashed away somewhere. In any event, I'm putting out an alert on this license plate.* Then his cell phone rang—Francesca's number—but when he answered it, there was no one there. Listening closely, though, he could hear voices in the background. There were sounds of chairs scraping and people arguing. He thought he heard someone say, "Just sit down and do what I say."

Something is definitely wrong. Where the hell is she?

Tony grabbed the keys to his police car. He'd try the church first, and see if her car was there. Just as he was leaving, he was stopped by John McNally, one of the other investigators.

"Hey, Viscardi, you look like you're in a major hurry, but I have news on the Cambio case."

"Can't it wait?" Tony was growing more certain by the second that Francesca was in trouble.

"Sure, but wait until you hear . . ."

Tony glanced frantically at his watch. "Look, I got another fire to put out, so let's talk later."

"Where you off to?"

"Saint Rita's—I have a suspicion Cambio's brother is over there, causing trouble."

"You need backup?"

"Right now, no, but I'll keep you posted." And with that, Tony went racing to his car.

* * * *

"*You* killed your brother, didn't you?" Sister Therese's voice rang out angrily in the room, which seemed to be growing increasingly stuffy. Francesca sat quietly, wishing Sister wouldn't provoke Chuck because he seemed to be on a very short fuse.

"Me? Hell, no! *You're* the main suspect, *Sister*." He spat out the final word as if it were a curse.

Sister's lips trembled, and Father Bunt clasped his hands, as if in prayer.

"Why in the world would you accuse *me* of murder?" Sister clutched the big crucifix attached to the rosary beads on her waist.

Chuck kept the gun pointed in their general direction as he spoke. "You can ask Francesca over there. She figured it out."

Francesca cringed as Sister Therese looked at her with an expression of outrage and sorrow.

"Oh, Sister, I'm so sorry. I don't know what to think now . . . but I noticed you had requested a Mass for Chip—for the repose of his soul—but it was before he actually died."

Francesca toyed nervously with the miraculous medal she wore on a chain around her neck. "But it wasn't just that, Sister. I . . . I saw you and Chip, a few months ago, on the school playground—and you were having a really violent argument. You looked like you wanted to kill him right then."

She saw Sister running her fingers tenderly over the figure affixed to the crucifix. The nun's words jolted Francesca's heart like lightning.

"And that evidence was enough for you to conclude that I *did* kill him?"

"What else *would* she conclude?" Chuck interjected. "It's the truth, isn't it?"

"The truth, if you want to know it," Sister said quietly, "is that I *did* request a Mass for him, but it wasn't for the repose of his soul. It was for his special intentions, because I was worried about him—and I thought he needed special graces."

"Special graces, my foot," Chuck said rudely. "So how do you figure the Mass book had him down as dead?"

Sister looked at Chuck as if he were a fourth-grader who had just butchered a basic word in a spelling bee. She spoke clearly and slowly: "The volunteer who wrote the information in the book must have made a mistake. It's as simple as that."

"Yeah, well, you had plenty of run-ins with him, didn't you?" Chuck asked.

"Yes, just like plenty of other people in the parish." Here she gave Francesca a particularly scathing look. "And I'll admit we did have a heated argument that day, but it was about baseball, for Heaven's sake, nothing serious!"

"Baseball?" Francesca asked weakly.

"Yes, I'm a big Braves fan, and Chip followed the Marlins." She rolled her eyes. "The *Marlins*."

Chuck was silent. Francesca could see the wheels spinning in his brain. She figured it was obvious to him that Sister was telling the truth. She felt terrible for ever having suspected Sister in the first place. *Oh, what a fool I've been. God, forgive me.* And she felt far worse for having been dumb enough to trust Chuck. *Is he the killer?*

"We're wasting time here," Chuck said. "This isn't a jury. I didn't come here to put anyone on trial for Chip's death. I have other fish to fry."

He pulled out a crumpled piece of paper from his pocket. "Chip sent me this to show me where he'd hidden some . . . some things I'm supposed to pick up."

The stolen chalices and crucifixes, Francesca thought.

"Anyway, I thought this was a map of the convent," Chuck continued. "There's what looks like a nun sketched over here."

He stopped and licked his lips nervously. "My brother was terrible at drawing. Look, all I want is someone to take me to the place where he hid the goods—and then I'm out of here."

He thrust the map into Father Bunt's hands. "Father, it's really convenient *you* showed up, since you're the CEO around here. I'll bet you can figure out this map."

Father Bunt turned the paper over a few times. Francesca noticed that his hands were trembling.

"What's this all about?"

"For God's sake!" Chuck was growing increasingly agitated. "It shows where Chip hid the gold cups and crosses and candlesticks and all that."

Now Chuck stood up and brandished the pistol alarmingly close to Father Bunt's head. "Look, I don't have all day, so don't play dumb with me."

* * * *

Tony had the cell phone pressed to his hear as he ran to his car. The sounds were garbled, but he could tell Francesca was with Father Bunt, Sister Therese, and someone else whose voice he couldn't identify. It sounded like Chip Cambio, though. *Could it be the brother?*

His emotions were an odd jumble: anger at Francesca for getting herself into what looked like big trouble; concern that she might be injured, or worse; and relief at finally making some headway on the case. *The brother could be the key to solving the whole thing.*

* * * *

Father Bunt decided not to agitate the man any further. Even for those valuable and sacred items it would be foolish to jeopardize three human lives.

He straightened out the wrinkled sheet of paper and studied it for a few moments. "This sketch is the statue of Mary in the rose garden. And I think I know where the . . . uh . . . stuff is hidden. It's just a short walk from here."

"Is there another way out of the convent?" Chuck asked Sister. "I don't want the sister at the reception desk to notice anything strange."

She nodded. "The back door is just down the hall."

"Now we're getting somewhere," Chuck said. "I tell you what, let's all four of us take a nice walk, shall we?" He pointed the gun to indicate that he wanted them to precede him out the door.

Father Bunt led the group at a rapid clip to the rose garden in the back of the church property. A few yards from a statue of Mary holding the Christ Child was a shed where the gardener kept his tools. Father Bunt mentioned to no one in particular that Chip evidently hadn't been very skilled at drawing. The proportions of the sketch made the shed seem much bigger than it actually was.

When they arrived there, Father Bunt was startled to see Dopey asleep right in the entryway of the shed. As they approached, the big dog stood up and wagged his tail fervently but continued blocking the door.

"Get that damn dog out of the way," Chuck muttered.

"Here, Dopey, come here, boy," Francesca crooned, but the dog just stayed put.

Chuck seemed to be growing increasingly more nervous, Father Bunt noticed. *Probably afraid the police are going to show up any minute—and I hope someone does.* But then he noted with horror that Chuck was pointing the gun straight at the dog.

Dopey let out a low warning growl.

"If that stupid mutt doesn't get out of the way, I'll shoot it," Chuck announced.

The two women seemed frozen with fear, and Father Bunt realized that the man was indeed crazy enough to kill the dog rather than try to gently remove it. But although the dog got on his nerves, there was no way he would allow Dopey to be injured. God had charged him with protecting the entire flock of Saint Rita's, and, in this case, that included Dopey. Besides, if the man was crazy enough to shoot a dog, he could turn his gun on anyone who got in his way, including Francesca, Sister, and Father Bunt himself. *Chuck called me the CEO of this place. Time I started acting like it.*

Father Bunt stood in front of Dopey. "Listen, I've had enough of this. How dare you threaten a poor animal?"

"Get out of the way, Father, I mean it."

"Look, it's time you listened to reason. This whole situation has gotten way out of hand. Let me go into the shed and I'll find the stuff for you." *If I can distract him, maybe I can get that gun away from him.*

But Chuck had a frantic look on his face. Father Bunt cringed as Chuck pointed the gun directly at him and shouted: "Get the hell out of the way!"

There was a far-off sound of sirens. Chuck turned his head sharply, and Father Bunt saw his moment and lunged at the gun. The Father Bunt heard a loud explosion and felt a searing hot pain in his arm. That was the last thing he recalled before blacking out.

* * * *

Francesca screamed as Father Bunt collapsed onto the ground. She then saw Sister Therese rush over to him and feel for a pulse.

"He's alive, thank God!" Sister then gently checked his arm. "But he's bleeding heavily. Somebody call 911!"

Francesca turned to Chuck. "How could you do this? What's wrong with you?"

She couldn't quite read his expression. He looked angry but also shocked and scared.

"I thought it was unloaded," he said.

For just a moment she glimpsed the man who had seemed so endearing in the coffee shop.

But that moment was over quickly, and Chuck turned to the women and yelled at them. "No one calls 911! No one calls anyone! You understand?"

Francesca had pulled the cell phone from her pocket, but now he grabbed it from her and hurled it into the undergrowth. Dopey had been scared off by the sound of the gun, so Chuck had no obstacle in his way now. The padlock on the old shed had been left open. He yanked open the door and motioned the two women inside.

"Get moving, you two! I'm not letting you out of my sight."

As she and Sister huddled together in a corner of the shed, Chuck pawed through the piles of old tools and bags that were stashed in a corner. When he hoisted a large bag with a clanking sound, she heard him say, "Finally!" She could see him looking into the bag and no doubt spying what he had come for.

He slung the bag over his shoulder and waved the gun again. "All right, you two, I'm going to lock you in here for a while."

"But what about Father?" Sister pleaded. "We have to get him help."

"Someone will come along eventually. Now shut up and stay still."

He exited the shed and closed the door roughly behind him. Francesca heard him putting the padlock on the door. The two women were left in darkness. Sister Therese began fiddling with her beads.

"Hail Mary, full of grace, the Lord is with thee."

* * * *

Tony heard a gunshot as he pulled up at Saint Rita's. He called for backup and then ran from the car with his gun drawn. The sound seemed to be coming from somewhere behind the rectory. As Tony approached the shed, he saw the man who had to be Cambio's twin coming out, carrying a bag and a gun, and Tony spun for cover behind a tree. A few seconds later the man hurried past the tree toward a car parked on the side of the road. Tony stalked him carefully, then raised his gun and yelled, "Police! Drop the gun!" At that precise moment, three cop cars, lights flashing, pulled up around the rectory driveway, and the officers came out, armed and running. In seconds, they had the man in custody.

Just then, Tony heard someone shouting. Two women, it sounded like. He took off running in their direction.

* * * *

Father Bunt slowly came to consciousness, but all he could see was blackness. He was aware of a terrible pain in his arm and a sticky wetness on his shirt sleeve. *I've been shot. And I'm blind!*

Then his eyes slowly began to focus. He realized that he wasn't blind after all. The blackness was just Dopey's large nose looming just inches from his face. The dog had that stupid tongue lolling out with drool dripping down. He could feel slobber raining on his chin.

The dog barked, but Father noticed that something sounded different. "W-w-w-woof!"

The poor, frightened animal had developed a stutter.

* * * *

Maria was rolling out pie dough in the rectory kitchen, when she heard a loud explosion outside and then a few moments later saw police cars arriving. She quickly wiped the flour and bits of lard from her hands and started outside, only to be met by Father William coming down the stairs. She noticed that his hair was sticking out every which way. *Must have been napping.* Father William looked frightened.

"I think someone shot Father Bunt. I saw the commotion from my window."

"Shot him! Who?"

Father William hurried toward the front door. "Well, I know this sounds crazy, but the guy sure looked like Chip."

Maria clasped her hand to her mouth. "It's that ghost, Father—Chip's ghost!"

* * * *

As he reached the shed, Tony saw Father Bunt lying, dazed, on the ground.

"I'm getting you help, don't worry," he said and put in a call for an ambulance.

Then Tony turned his attention to opening the padlock. He shouted, "Police! I'm gonna shoot the padlock open, so stand back away from the door! Do you hear me?" There was a muffled reply in the affirmative. Tony counted out loud to three and fired once, obliterating the latch the padlock was attached to. He then pulled open the door and rushed inside. In the darkness he could barely make out the figures of Sister Therese and Francesca, huddled together in the far corner. When he called her name, Francesca ran straight for Tony and threw herself into his arms. She was sobbing.

"What about Father?" Sister Therese asked, as the three of them made their way out of the shed. Francesca was leaning heavily against Tony, as if the shock had weakened her. He saw an ambulance pulling up and men with a stretcher heading for Father Bunt.

"I'm sure he'll be fine. Now let's get the two of you inside so you can sit down."

As they neared the rectory, Maria and Father William came rushing over. Tony couldn't quite understand what Maria was saying, but she kept using the word "ghost." Father William gently took Sister Therese's arm.

"Let me help you inside, Sister, you've been through quite an ordeal."

In the rectory kitchen, Francesca sat down wearily with Sister Therese next to her. She could see her own shock mirrored on the nun's face. Meanwhile, Maria bustled around, getting them both cups of tea and putting out some freshly baked lemon cookies. Francesca bit into a cookie absently, grateful to be alive. She noticed that Tony was going out of his way to take care of her. He kept asking her if she wanted anything else. But what she really wanted was to push the rewind button on her life so she would never have gotten mixed up with Chuck. *What a fool I was to trust him! And now I'll have to tell Tony that I agreed to Chuck's plot.*

CHAPTER 15

Father Bunt awakened the next morning in a strange bed. The sheets were rough and the mattress felt like it was made of stone. An acrid, antiseptic aroma permeated the air. He had very little memory of how he had arrived there. *This has to be a hospital.* His bandaged arm was stiff and very sore, and he felt as if he had been in a fight. Every muscle in his body was aching. He remembered falling after he was shot. *That's why I'm so sore.*

He went over the events in his mind. Somehow, Chip's twin brother must have been in on the heist at the church all along. But did the man kill his own brother? Was he capable of murder? Sister Therese had called Father Bunt the night before, reporting that Chuck had said he thought the gun had not been loaded. Did Chuck really believe that? *I wonder if it's true*. Maybe, after the gun fired, the man realized he'd be facing a stiff prison sentence, so he pretended he was more bark than bite. Bark. That reminded him of poor Dopey. *I hope he's over the trauma by now.*

Father Bunt examined the plastic bracelet on his wrist. He was in DeKalb Medical Center, very near Saint Rita's. He had never been hospitalized before, except for that time long ago when he was ten and he'd had his tonsils removed. His mother had promised him he'd be able to eat all the ice cream he wanted after the surgery, but he'd been so nauseated and in so much pain, he couldn't eat anything at all.

A nurse bustled in the door, wearing a pink-and-white flower-print outfit, which made him wonder what had happened to the old-fashioned, crisp white uniforms that had once been standard. Was the medical profession doing what so many nuns had done—ditching the regulation uniform? But why would nurses want to wear outfits that looked like pajamas?

The woman smiled at him and patted his hand as if he were a child. She looked to be in her early twenties, plump with sleek, butter-yellow hair and eyes that seemed too blue to be real. They were outlined with a thick black liner that gave her the look of a friendly blonde raccoon.

"You look like you're feeling a lot better, Mr. Bunt." Her voice had the singsong intonations one would use with a four-year-old.

"Er, actually, I'm Father Bunt. You see, I'm a priest—the pastor of Saint Rita's Catholic Church."

The woman looked stunned. *Probably never met a priest before.*

"Catholic," she said with a look on her face as if he'd mentioned space aliens. "Well, do tell. We had some Catholic neighbors back home in Birmingham. They were just the nicest people—Mexicans!" Now she clucked her tongue. "But they had so many children!"

She studied him. "You don't look Mexican, Mr. . . . er . . . Father Bunt."

He tried to adjust the paper-covered pillow behind his head. *Is it made of wood?*

"Uh, well, no, I'm not. I'm actually of German descent."

She shrugged, as if the mystery were too much for her. Then she gave the rigid pillow a sharp punch, looked at his chart, and made a few notes.

"Well, my name is Mabel Brown, Father. I'm just an Alabama girl, born and bred. That's all. I go to the big Baptist church right over there on Clairmont Avenue."

She suddenly turned and looked out the door into the hall. "Oh, you have a visitor. Are you feeling up to seeing someone?"

Father Bunt tried to sit up but winced in pain. He managed to pull his pajama jacket more tightly around his chest and made an effort to comb his hair with his fingers. But every move created searing sensations in his arm. *I probably look exactly like I feel. I hope it's William.* But when he looked up, he discovered his visitor was none other than Archbishop MacPherson.

* * * *

Tony was in Francesca's kitchen, making her a pot of tea, while she sat on the couch with Tubs on her lap. The old cat was purring contentedly, completely unaware of all the terrible things that had happened the day before. Francesca stroked his fur lovingly. *Sometimes I wish I were a cat.*

But then Tony came into the room with such a look of concern in his eyes. He put the tea pot down on the coffee table along with a handful of ginger nut cookies he'd found in the cookie jar. Then he pulled up a chair next to her. She was basking in all his attention, but there was that terrible sense of guilt that kept scratching at the back of her mind, like a persistent cat trying to get out a door. *I have to tell him about Chuck. He's going to find out, sooner or later, and I'd much rather he knew from me.*

"You OK?" He handed her a cup of tea and gently pushed back a strand of hair from her forehead.

She nodded, sipped the tea, and then stroked Tubs, stalling for time.

"There are a lot of things I haven't told you about the case," he said. "I was just getting some news when all this happened, and I went running out of the station. But there've been some rather interesting developments."

"Oh?" She knew now was the time. She knew she should tell him. So why was she keeping silent? *Because if I tell him, I'll lose him for good.*

He pulled out his cell phone. "That reminds me. Let me call the station."

She sat quietly sipping her tea while he dialed the number. *Please, God, give me the courage to tell him the truth.*

* * * *

Father Bunt tried desperately to get out of bed so he could greet the archbishop properly.

"Stay put. Don't move a muscle." The archbishop's voice rang with finality. "Your job right now is to rest and get well. Let's put formalities aside."

Father Bunt lay back, relieved. Getting out of bed would have been impossible anyway.

The archbishop found a chair and pulled it closer to the bed. Father Bunt noticed that the expression on his face was far less threatening and less disappointed than the last time they had met.

"Brent, good news: the doctors say you're going to be fine."

At that moment, the nurse in the flower-print pajamas entered the room. The archbishop stood and introduced himself, mentioning the Catholic Archdiocese of Atlanta.

"It's a pleasure to meet you, sir." She did a little curtsey. "My name is Mabel Brown." Then she paused. "Are *you* Mexican, sir?"

* * * *

After a short conversation, Tony put the cell phone back in his pocket. He sat down on the couch. "I have to say, this case is really getting stranger and stranger."

Francesca felt her stomach twinge with anxiety. *Does he know about me and Chuck?*

"What do you mean, stranger?"

"Well, it doesn't look like the twin . . . what's his name . . . Chuck . . . was involved in Chip's death at all."

Tony looked at her with an expression she hadn't seen before. It made her nervous.

"Francesca, Chuck Cambio gave us a full confession about the thefts at the church. It seems he and Chip were working together to embezzle the building fund, plus steal a few valuable items. The mother and sister were in on it, too. They were supposed to sell the stolen goods, and the brothers were going to split the cash and get out of the country. But Chip's death changed everything." Tony took a bite of the cookie.

"After that, the women got greedy and decided they wanted the money for themselves, so they came looking for the key to the safety-deposit box before Chuck could find it. Chuck was planning to head back to Florida and confront them about the key, but first he wanted to get the other things."

He looked at her with a quizzical expression. "Isn't there something you want to tell me? About you and Chuck?"

The old cat seemed to encourage her by meowing loudly. She put down her cup of tea and sat up straighter. "Yes, Tony, there is."

* * * *

The nurse checked Father Bunt's temperature and pulse and took his blood pressure, while the archbishop busied himself at the window, checking e-mail on his BlackBerry. Then she gave Father Bunt a glass of juice, made a few more notes on the chart, and left the room. Father Bunt sipped the juice and waited for whatever came next. The straw, he noticed, was purple, and the cup had little dancing elephants printed on it. *I wonder if they put me in the children's ward by mistake.*

The archbishop put away the BlackBerry, walked back over to the chair, and sat down again.

"Brent, I stopped by to let you know that I am *very*, *very* . . ."

Here it comes. Father Bunt gripped the elephant-imprinted cup and readied himself for the worst.

"... *proud* of you for the way you handled things. I've had a full report about the way you *took charge* and protected the lives of those two women."

Father Bunt had nearly crumpled the cup, he was so surprised. "Thank you, Your Grace, but, really, I . . ."

"Don't be modest. There are very few men with that kind of courage."

Now MacPherson stood up and gazed out the window. "But that isn't the only reason I'm here. I also wanted to share the police report with you. There's some very good news on that front as well."

Father Bunt put the juice cup down. *More good news. Is this a dream?*

MacPherson continued looking out the window as he spoke. In the distance, Father Bunt heard an ambulance shrieking and then a chorus of dogs chiming in. He wondered if Dopey was howling back at home.

The archbishop walked over to the window and adjusted the blinds. Then he turned to face Father Bunt. "Yes, it seems that *all* the money and *all* the stolen goods have been returned to the parish. The liturgist was working in tandem with a twin brother, it seems, and the mother and sister were involved as well. The police got confessions from them all."

"And the murderer?" Father Bunt was still horrified at the thought that one brother had killed another.

"There *was* no murderer. Well, not in the ordinary sense, anyway."

* * * *

Francesca knew there was no use avoiding the topic any further. "Tony, I'm so sorry. You're going to be really angry when I tell you . . ."

He stood up and walked across the room. He seemed to be looking at a book on her shelves, or maybe he was stalling for time. He turned around and faced her.

"I promise not to be angry. I just need to know the truth."

His face looks so stern. This is it—he'll go running out of here and never return. But I have to tell him.

It took her a few minutes to tell him how she had met Chuck and how she had agreed to keep his identity a secret.

"Tony, he seemed, well, legitimate, you know? Really concerned about his brother." She avoided his eyes. "Was he just a scam artist? And was that all Chip was, too?"

"Some of what you saw was true," Tony said. "Apparently Chip and his brother really did differ over religion—but one thing they agreed on was making a killing at Saint Rita's."

She sat quietly, trying to process the information.

"These things aren't black and white," Tony said. "I've seen enough crimes in my time to know you can have a guy who seems to be the perfect family man, but he's also bilking his company out of thousands of dollars. And there's the mother who's devoted to her kids, but she's selling drugs on the side." He paused.

"In this case, it looks like Chip really did think he was doing Saint Rita's some good with all the changes he was making. He really believed in those dumb songs and the Stations of the Earth, and all the rest of it. But at the exact same time, he was planning the theft."

"As for Chuck," Tony continued, "he did want to find out who had killed his brother—but he also wanted to cash in on the stolen goods."

Her heart was beating very quickly. She remembered how she had been taken in by Chuck's apparent earnestness. How she had even accepted a date with him. She thought of his condo and how bare it had been. *It was all like a stage set for a play. And when I showed up that day, so unexpectedly, I walked right into his plot.*

This is it. I have to tell Tony. And so she nervously divulged her plan to confront Sister and get her to confess to the murder.

"Why Sister Therese?" Tony asked

"Well, for one, she had a really hot temper when it came to Chip." Then she explained about the Mass book, as well as the day she had seen Chip and Sister arguing on the playground.

She sniffed nervously. "I just jumped to the wrong conclusion."

He stood there, silently. She could tell he was trying to control his temper. Then he sat down next to her.

"Francesca, do you know how dangerous your secret plot could have been? Do you realize that people could have died because of it?"

She began to cry. Of course, he was right. Tubs looked up at her, as if startled by the sudden hot raindrops that were splattering against his fur.

"But Tony, I tried to call you—before I went over to visit Sister."

"Yes, but why didn't you let me know about Chuck sooner? That way, I might have prevented everything that happened—and Father Bunt wouldn't be in the hospital now." He walked over to the window and looked out into the yard.

"Did you and Chuck . . . go out?"

She felt stricken with guilt as she remembered Chuck's invitation to dinner. "Oh, just for coffee, nothing more, although . . ."

"Although?"

"Well, he did invite me out to dinner, and . . ."

"And you said yes." Tony was still looking out the window. She suddenly realized Tony thought something serious had developed between her and Chuck.

"Yes, I did. He just seemed . . . well, he seemed nice, and you and I weren't really talking. But Tony, believe me, there was nothing between us."

Tony nodded. Then he walked over and faced her. His expression was very serious. "You had important information I could have used on the case, Francesca. Why did you wait so long to contact me?"

"I didn't think you'd listen to me. I knew you'd just tell me to keep my nose out of everything. And . . . and . . . well, I thought if I could help you with the investigation, you and I would get back together again." She hesitated. "A crazy plan, I admit, but it seemed logical at the time. You see, I thought it was over between us. I thought . . ." She broke down again.

"Over? How could you get that idea?"

"We had that fight . . ." Her voice trailed off.

Now he looked sad. "One disagreement and it's over?"

She shrugged. What could she say?

He sat down next to her. "We had a fight. That's all. And for that I owe you an apology."

She moved closer to him on the couch. "No, it was my fault. You were right—there are all these reminders of Dean everywhere. The place really is like a shrine . . ."

He put his arm around her shoulders. "It's fine, Francesca."

He pulled her very close to him. She could feel the lovely scratchy feeling of his face against hers. "I'll be patient. Just don't call it quits between us so easily, OK?"

Now the tears came in a big storm. He caught a teardrop on his finger. "Hey, Tubs is going to need a towel if you keep this up."

This made her smile, and then she started to laugh. "You'll forgive me, then?"

She put Tubs down, and they both rose from the couch. He took her in his arms and held her very tightly against him. She knew her tears were wetting his shirt.

"You got it."

* * * *

Maria was in the kitchen with Sister Therese when Father William stopped by, carrying the aquarium with Ignatius inside. He planned to visit a lady at the nursing home who loved hamsters. But when he realized there were freshly baked cookies, he stopped in for a few moments, placing the aquarium on a small table in the corner of the kitchen and assuring Maria that the hamster, sound asleep, would not bother her.

Maria had purchased a get-well card for Father Bunt for all of them to sign. She also had made a batch of chocolate-chip cookies with extra pecans and a double dose of vanilla, which was just the way he liked them. But she noticed Father

William eyeing the platter of cookies, so she allowed him to have one. She also gave one to Sister. Then Maria brought up the topic that had been bothering her ever since Chip's brother had been arrested.

"You know what the rumors are, don't you?"

"What rumors?" Sister Therese looked up from the card she was signing.

Maria reached over absently and selected a cookie. She could make another batch for Father Bunt tomorrow. She had all the ingredients. She bit into the cookie, noting the vanilla was just right.

"They're saying it wasn't a murder after all . . . Chip's death."

"Who's they?" Father William asked, selecting a second cookie.

"Oh, Father, you know—they. I don't know who they are." She sat down at the table and picked up the card Sister had just signed. Maria had chosen one with a dog on the front that resembled Dopey. She knew how fond Father was of the dog, even if he wouldn't admit it.

Maria was just about to continue the conversation, when the kitchen door inched open, and Dopey entered. He was accompanied by another, much smaller dog.

"Isn't that Chip's dog?" Father William asked.

Maria smiled at the two dogs. "Yes, that's Wormwood, but I call him Woody, bless his heart. We're keeping him here until we find him a home. And it looks like he and Dopey have become buddies."

She stood up and rushed over to the cupboard, and came back with dog biscuits shaped like a mailman. She handed one to Woody and then one to Dopey. The biscuits were demolished quickly in the dogs' mouths. Then Father William went over to the aquarium and held a piece of biscuit near the mountain of litter. In seconds, a small face with trembling whiskers poked out, and Ignatius accepted the morsel.

* * * *

The archbishop picked up the empty elephant-print cup and examined it as if it were an ancient artifact. Father Bunt wondered if MacPherson were actually seeing it or just playing with it the way people sometimes toy with paper clips when they are lost in thought.

"Why elephants, I wonder," the archbishop said.

"Uh, it does seem unusual." Father Bunt tried to get comfortable in the bed. *I wish he would cut to the chase. The suspense is getting to me. Plus, I could use a bathroom break.*

The archbishop put the cup down. "Well, here is the really strange part. It seems a number of odd things happened that night. The subway tremors had caused the bolts on the shelves, over time, to loosen from the wall. That night, a train nearly derailed, causing a particularly strong tremor. And the police believe that Chip was standing on a stepladder, reaching for a book, when two things happened: one, there was the tremor, and two, something brushed against him, causing him to lose his balance. And since his hand was on the shelf, and since the shelves were unsteady, he more or less pulled the whole thing down on himself."

"But what brushed against him?"

"What's the name of that dog in the rectory again?"

Father Bunt sat up in bed, forgetting momentarily about the pain in his arm. "Dopey?"

"That's right! Dopey. They found dog hairs at the scene, matching Dopey's, and they think he came in and . . . accidentally, of course . . . bumped into the stepladder."

Father Bunt drummed his fingers on the little table near his bed. "That's strange, though. You see, Dopey hardly ever roams around at night. He was sound asleep that evening when I left him."

Now Father Bunt took a deep breath. "Unless . . ."

MacPherson raised an eyebrow. "Unless?"

"Well, he must have been chasing Ignatius."

The eyebrow went up higher. "Ignatius?"

"The hamster."

* * * *

When Maria got to the part about Dopey, Sister Therese sat up straighter in her chair. "So this means it wasn't murder after all," Sister said. "It was really an accident, wasn't it?"

Father William helped himself to a third cookie. "Well, given that the shelves were loosened by vibrations from the train, and given Dopey's involvement, maybe 'accident' isn't quite the correct term."

Sister patted her chocolate-stained lips with a paper napkin. "Well, what would be better?"

* * * *

After the archbishop had left, Father Bunt looked at the supper tray with dismay. He hadn't been hospitalized for a stomach ailment, so why were they feeding him what looked like baby food? Mashed potatoes, some kind of smashed vegetable, which could be a carrot or a sweet potato, and that brown thing in the corner. He nudged it with his fork. It was some kind of meat that had been ground so fine, it was almost liquid. But he was hungry, so he cleaned the plate and then examined the gelatin dessert. He prodded the little orange cubes with his fork and watched them quiver. *If this has become entertainment, I'm definitely ready to go home.*

Then he sat back and sighed contentedly. All in all, it had been a fine day. A visit from the archbishop, who had told him that all the stolen goods and money had been restored to the parish. And the best news of all: there really hadn't been a murder at Saint Rita's after all.

He smiled as he remembered the way the archbishop had put it.

"The death of the liturgist was simply an act of God."

About the Author

Lorraine V. Murray is the author of *Abbess of Andalusia: Flannery O'Connor's Spiritual Journey*, *Grace Notes*, *Why Me? Why Now?*, *Confessions of an Ex-Feminist*, and a mystery novel, *Death in the Choir*. She's also a columnist with the *Atlanta Journal-Constitution* and the *Georgia Bulletin*, and works part-time at the Pitts Theology Library at Emory University. Lorraine and her husband, Jef, live in Decatur, Georgia, and are parishioners at St. Thomas More Catholic Church. Her Web site is www.lorrainevmurray.com.